Dracula's Son

by

J. W. Keleher

Published by J. W. Keleher

Copyright © 2022 by J. W. Keleher

Discover other titles by J. W. Keleher at JWKeleher.com

All rights reserved, including the right of reproduction in whole or in part in any form.

Table of Contents

Chapter 1: The Decision 1

Chapter 2: Frog Dreams 13

Chapter 3: The Escape 23

Chapter 4: My New Life 40

Chapter 5: Healing 48

Chapter 6: Spring Strength 56

Chapter 7: The Cleansing 60

Chapter 8: High Meadow 68

Chapter 9: Summer Market 79

Chapter 10: Skinny Sheep 93

Chapter 11: Truth 113

To those who choose love over fear.

"We will take half of your flock. The protection and leadership in this kingdom do not come without a price." Lancu's mouth, like a slice in a hog's thigh, grins with black teeth and gummy spaces. One of his ring-covered hands directs a group of boys into our corral. With the other, he pushes me against the fence. I lose my footing and slip onto the duff and dung increasing the holes in my leggings, but my mind is elsewhere.

I picture it. With a sword, I could sever his pumpkin-shaped head from his fat body. Yes, it would be easy. My thoughts end with the beasts' clatter-by in a mix of dust and oily sheep smell. I pull myself up on my staff. "It will take us years to build our flock again. The drought has people hungering everywhere—even here in the mountains. Why must you take so much? We have known hunger but never as now and still there is winter ahead."

"I cannot take pity on every shepherd in Wallachia. Your welfare is not my concern. It is simple, shepherd, you must pay your taxes or suffer the consequences," Lancu sneers as he spits out the words.

My ears turn red as I fill with anger. I want to swing my staff and end Lancu's arrogance. My hand clutches the smoothed wood of my staff until my knuckles turn red. I am ready!

Tata must have read my mind, behind and off to the side of Lancu, his head shakes just so and very slightly. I stand up straight and glared at my greatest enemy, "Let us be friends". He and his soldiers laugh in response like a group of crows. I take a deep breath and loosen my grip. I further brush the dirt from my leggings to distract my mind.

The young herders dare not glance at me. They focus on driving the sheep down the hill with the help of their lanky hounds. Petra lays at Mama Tudora's feet growling and with raised eyes asks me what he should do. I pat downward in the air with my hand to signal for him to stay.

"We will be back next year. I'll want to see fatter sheep!" Lancu insults me further by spitting at my feet. He pulls the length of his embroidered cloak around waiting for me to take action. His nod sends the guards off, but his eyes stay on mine. I could jump on him--maybe break his neck before the soldiers pull me away.

Tata steps behind me. His throat clears. Yes, Tata, I know what you expect me to say. My eyes search deep into Lancu's and I swear I can see his soul. It is so very dark. My anger changes somehow magically to pity. I speak with sincerity, "Let us be friends."

His laugh rolls off into the forest and a playful pair of rabbits scamper off under the shelter of a bush. "Voicu, you are as weak as one of your sheep. Phaah! Why do I bother?" As he turns to join his entourage, a shift of wind blows his cloak up exposing the shine of a hidden dagger in his hand. He meant to kill me.

Mama Tudora sits on a stool near the house and cries into her folded arms, "How can we survive? Even the forest appears barren. Even wild carrots and turnips are sparse. Everything is dry waste. Our flock is small and we must help them to survive too. How can we do this? How?"

Tata Gigore kneels down and strokes her hand to bring some calm. "Now, now, Mama. Have faith. We will struggle. It will be a difficult winter but we have each other. With love and faith, all things are possible."

"Voicu! Voicu!" Dumitra galloped down the hill. The bow and quiver at her sides bounce with the wave of her long raven-shine hair. To go from my greatest enemy to my greatest love so quickly reminds me of being a boy–I would spin endlessly and then fall on soft grass watching the world tilt until God made it right. She bounds up to me.

I circle my arm around my wife with a hug and kiss. I whisper in her ear and she nods with a smile. We hold hands as we step over to Tata and Mama. I clear my throat, "Not all is barren." I place my hand on Dumitra's belly.

Mama's eyes grow wide and she jumps up wiping the tears from her eyes. "Oh! Oh! Oh! You two make me so happy!" She embraces Dumitra and then pulls me into the hug along with a kiss. "How could you keep this from us? Oh, I have prayed so for you to have a child. Now I will be a grandmamma! Oh, I must get started to prepare for this child."

"But Mama you are not having the child," I explained.

"Oh, you men. How could you understand? Dumitra will need my help along the way. I have acted as a midwife often. So, Dumitra, let us go begin our preparations." She takes Dumitra by the hand and my wife smiles with a shrug as they wander off into the woods.

Tata takes a pipe out of his satchel. "Come, Son. We too must visit." He puts his arm around my shoulder as we amble over toward the sheep corral. We lean on the fence. He lights the pipe and, in turn, we fill our lungs with the mix of herbs. "We too must make our plans. I know Voicu that we will suffer much. I will do everything I can to keep our family fed and protected. Maybe losing some of our flock is a good thing. We will be challenged feeding the ones we still have," Tata shared and then took another puff from the pipe. "We will survive somehow. You must make certain Dumitra eats for herself and the child she carries. If this winter takes one of us, it should be me. I have lived a good life."

"Yes, Tata. I will make certain my wife eats. But, you must not think I will allow you to sacrifice yourself. If any should have died long ago, it is I. Our tax collector intended to take my life today, but here I am. It is because of the love in our family. This is, I believe, how we will find our way through the coming winter. Love will not allow any of us to slip away to heaven. This I know. Love is powerful!" I smile and Tata hands the pipe to me again.

Then there is a rustling along the mountain path. Someone is coming. It is Dumitra's father Barbu the Bear. He is a man who lives up to his reputation of strength, size, and determination. His dark hair and beard are like a wooly curse forced upon a gentle face. "How do you fare?" asks Barbu as he approaches Tata and me..

"Lancu and his men just left. We are blessed with the weaker half of our flock," I explain.

"What? Why that demon! His only concern is to line his pockets with gold. Maybe his new Master will put him at the end of a stick!" Barbu growls through grit teeth.

"New Master?" Tata curls his lip and raises one eyebrow.

"You have not heard?" Barbu takes the pipe from Tata and refills it. Then he takes short puffs to get the embers going again. "Vlad Tepes is back in power. Dracula has returned."

I turn away. My heart races and my mind spins. This is unexpected news. How could it be? For years I had not heard his name- Dracula. I had thought his death must have happened long ago. My true father— Dracula. Maybe he could provide assistance to my family through the winter? Maybe he would have a sword thrust through me? I am confused. I must have time to think. An owl swoops overhead looking for a whisker twitch. It will be dark soon.

My wife returns from the forest, "Your face tells me you are burdened. Let me help." Dumitra moves closer and closer. She and Mama Tudora must have finished their talk. I glance at her, Tata Grigore and Tata Barbu. It is a still silent moment. Dracula is alive and in power. The cooling wind from the mountain carries the soft smell of my love. Dumitra strokes her hand across my cheek.

"I must go to the rock," for the first time I turn away from Dumitra to Tata. He has overheard and nods in approval still deep in conversation with Barbu. I stride off and Petra insists on following. Dumitra's eyes search the ground as though for the words she cannot find, as Mama takes her by the arm and guides her back to the house.

CHAPTER 1

The Decision

Tonight, I choose between truths and lies. I look above to the Shepherds' Star, as I sit on the rock and think of events and times. This is the place Tata Grigore taught me to go when I sought an answer. He has always told me, "The answer will come, Son. The answer will come." He is kind and fair. I call him Tata, though he is not my true father.

It seems only a dream; it is long ago. But, it is true. I am the son of Vlad Tepes also known as Dracula—the Son of the Dragon. He is the cruelest, most feared man in Romania and some say the world. The king of Hungary has released him from imprisonment and once again he is in power.

I am confused and some might wonder why. Why do I sit deep in thought? Why do I wait to take action? Save for the hard winter certain to lie ahead, I am happy in my life now. I am content. But God may have another purpose in mind for me. And how can I tell Dumitra? How will my family survive? I sit and think through my life--it has been both light and dark. It started in the dark. I remember my twelfth birthday and a feast in my honor. I was but a boy then and truly unkind. Kindness came with time. Kindness came.

To say I was spoiled and terrible described little of my ways. I slammed my hand on the nearest table or stomped on the floor as I ordered the servants. They were quick to respond to my requests. I spilled my drink on the table and one would wipe it clean. I yelled for

1

the door to open. The cool gust of wind swirled across my face and chilled my anger. I asked for something to eat and the pantry host arrived. Whether old or young, they hurried to obey my whims with a, "Yes, Young Master Mihnea."

"I do not like this." I threw the apple at the servant who placed it in my lap. Then I stood up from my chair with my hands on my hips. "Bring me a more comfortable chair." The girl ran off and returned an instant later. I tested the seat with my hand. "It must be softer!" I pointed her to the door. "Yes, Young Master Mihnea." Off she scampered soon to return with a pillow filled with soft goose feathers. "Yes." I sat. "This is more fitting."

One group in the castle, the soldiers and guards, did not follow my wishes and this struck me as odd. I heard mooted screams from beyond a gate, door, or down in the dungeon and the guards would always block my entry. "These are your father's orders," they would say. And I was never allowed outside of the castle gates or even to view beyond the reach of the chamber windows. "Young Mihnea, your parents do not wish you outside. My orders are to keep you safe inside." Sir Stephan, one of the gate watchmen and guards, explained with a pat on my shoulder.

I did go on several trips outside of the walls with Mama. We left and returned in the dark of night. I crawled into the carriage asleep or very near. I had never viewed the castle from the outside.

But my birthday—oh, my birthday. I had thought twelve was so near being an adult. It was obvious. One of the royalty, like me, would be thrust into manhood with a sword or fighting spear.

Mama was seated on one side and Father on the other. I sat nearer to Mama and held her hand. She protected me. And, as I remember, she was the only person I knew who didn't fear Father.

"The boy does not need such a feast," She said looking straight at my father. Her long bangs hung like black silk over her eyes, and she combed them back with her long fingers.

"He is the son of Dracula. Why, woman, do you think he wouldn't need such humoring?" My father's neatly trimmed mustache bounced with his words as though having a life of its own.

"He is only twelve. Why not let him play with the other children?" she suggested.

"The other children fear him—as they should! He cannot afford to be weak. Would you have him become a woman for the Sultan—like my brother?" My father looked away.

Mother reached over me and grabbed my father's arm turning him towards her. "Do not look away from me, Vlad!" The attendant to my mother gasped and stepped back from the couple.

"Woman!" My father threw his glass of drink against the wall and it shattered into a hundred pieces. He stood and the table vibrated as he pounded it with each word. "I will not let this boy be weak! He must be a leader. If you shame me again, you will regret it. Do not think you hold such power over me!"

The hall was silent and still, save for the flicker from the candles. It was a long moment then the awkward hush ended. Servants appraised it was time to move again; eyes to the ground, they scurried to their duties.

Mama lowered her sight. She swallowed dry which made her throat slide; she would not speak so to my father again. She knew what could happen.

A minstrel group danced with jingling bells around their ankles and wrist. The few women were in long gowns which flowed with greens and blues. The men bounced in large hats with embroidered brims. They wore leggings with puffy striped tops of blue and white. They performed in front of the gathering. With smiles, they shook their bells and played their instruments. Then, with shiny teeth and merry eyes, they circled the head table and sang some cheerful tune.

I ignored them as they came close. I cared nothing for their music. My mind was thinking of a sword or lesser blade I had hoped for. I do not remember the words, but later they would sing into my nightmares.

Father turned to observe me as I watched them. I yawned. I heard the whistle from his nostrils as his face pulled close.

"Ah, my son. You look tired. Are you bored?" my father's mustache curled slightly as he grinned.

"Yes, Father, the music is dull." I leaned back and stretched my arms high.

"I agree. We will see if they can sing a different tune," he shared.

Then Father pushed his chair from the table and wandered stroking his chin. He spoke to one of his men at the door. The guard's eyes gleamed at the minstrels mischievously. Father laughed and slapped the man on the shoulder. Some cold breeze swept across my back and neck which caused me to shiver. What had Father said?

The guard marched up to the stage and spoke to the man plucking the lute. The lute player raised his hand and the group stopped. The minstrels jangled off to one side and then some guards formed a line behind them. The music makers looked at each other as several guards pushed them ahead. The bells jingled. One woman sobbed into her hand, as soldiers pushed them ahead and out. I laughed at their odd reactions to their forced leave.

Father clapped his hands with such force they hurt my ears. It was his signal to have the feast set up. The room became active. Servants ran about. They set up the food on the side tables and rushed to fill goblets with a drink. Some used their arms and sleeves to clear off the table tops. Servants carried bowls filled with fruit and plates of sweet-smelling meat pie. They appeared from doors in every direction.

"I have a surprise for you after dinner." Father smiled down at me. It made me unsettled. Somehow, I knew it was not a sword.

Mama put her hand over her mouth and pushed her plate away. "I am not so hungry."

"Eat!" Father commanded Mama as he pounded the table once more. "I will not have a wife with legs like a bird and a face long like a mule. Eat!"

I was surprised that Mama felt no hunger as a roasted boar was hefted onto our table. The smell of cooked turnips, onions, and garlic swirled through the air. The food was endless and tasty! I washed all of it down with some buttermilk. Then, I wiped my mouth on my sleeve. My thoughts were of pleasant sleep with a full belly, but this was not to be.

Father raised his goblet. "For my son. As he grows to a man, I give him the gift of strength, and wash away all his fear." His throat moved with the rhythm of each swallow like the contortions of the underside of a snake's belly. The red dribbled down his mustache to his chin as his lips curled into a smile. Others in the hall cheered and raised their drinks.

Mama was quiet and grabbed my hand with a squeeze under the table hidden from all eyes. She did not look in my direction. She was silent.

Those in attendance ate, drank, and had merry conversations. From time to time, one would nod in my direction and hold their goblet up toasting my birthday. It was my celebration and I would remember it. Yes, I would remember this night. It would haunt me for many years to come.

The conversations lightened. Plates were cleared away. Some still drank with laughter. I noticed both Mama and Father were silent. Father's chair legs made a kind of groan as he pushed them back and a servant hurried in to move the chair aside. Mama squeezed my hand once more away from seeing eyes and did not say a word. He nodded to me with a smile and beckoned me to rise.

My father took me by my other hand. "Now for your gift." I did not know what to think—a new horse? Maybe a sword. Yes, a sword. He knows this will make me happy. He led me out the main door. We rushed down the corridor filled with lighted torches. The flames caused our shadows to dance madly from wall to wall and out into the courtyard. Brilliant gray fogged light; I squinted as my eyes teared. A crow's flap, flap, flap. Was it a warning? Why was my heart kicking in my chest? Time stopped, as we stepped along on the slick stone walkway.

The guards at the door nodded and bowed to Father. "Someday, Son, you will rule this countryside. You cannot afford to be weak. Your greatest ally will not be other people. It will be fear."

As Father spoke, my first notice was the change in smell. The sweetness of the feast gave way to another scent--strong and bitter. Father sensed my weakness; he gripped my hand solid and dragged me in a stumbling step.

A group of guards stood in the circle of the courtyard and blocked our view of I knew not what. I saw only long poles reaching for the sky, above them.

"This is my birthday gift to you." Father pulled me along.

First I thought my eyes deceived me, as the guards stepped aside and opened their circle. On each pole was a body. Some balanced high in the air. Others dropped close to the ground. The poles had been thrust through these people. They were without clothes. And then I recognized them. The minstrels? Father pranced with me into the middle of them. I turned my eyes down, and he forced my head up. His large calloused hand held my chin. My breath was short and quick. My mouth was dry yet filled with bitter liquid from my guts. I tried to move my eyes away but the scene surrounded me. My throat tightened and it became hard to swallow. I felt like I was a boy spirit, looking down at a boy--looking at dead and dying people. Somehow, their appearance and movement reminded me of frogs. And, to myself, I thought—just think of them as frogs. They are frogs.

"Look, son, this is what fear looks like," The lute player's limbs jiggled. The pole came out of his mouth with a raspy breath. He was still alive. He grabbed at the air with fingers curling in an unending rhythm. And then his arms thrashed like a frog trying to swim upstream. His eyes bulged out. A soft gurgled sound of blood bubbled out of his mouth at the same pace as his chest grew and shrank. A frog—a frog that's all he is.

Then a deep rumble erupted from my stomach and I tasted an acidic belch. I turned away from my father. I threw up and the vomit came like rainwater off the roof with splashes onto my shoes and pants. He laughed. Then he led me on.

"They disappointed you. Do they sound better now?" He laughed again—deep and roaring. He shook and swung my hand as he smiled like one of the castle hounds dreaming of rabbit stew. Father guided me around and pointed to the bodies. "They are not afraid to die now. What they are afraid of now is to live."

I breathed more regularly with time. And, I admit, after a while, maybe a short time or maybe a long time, I became used to the smell and sights. Father ordered the guards to open the main gates. I had never been allowed to exit the castle. I thought of some openness, but this privilege came with a great cost.

Bodies on poles covered the hillside next to the castle. On and on they went in lines like God had planted a garden of death. I could not count so high!

"These are very fresh. Let us walk, so you can see how it is done. Someday God may give you the same task. Do not ignore my gift."

His hand felt like it was made of oak with veins and sinewy courses of muscle and tendon. I stumbled as I tried to control my footing and there was no choice but to go forward. In the low valley, more soldiers were assembled. They stood in a double row with the prisoners inside and pairs of horses at the end.

When we came to the line, my father said, "Make way! It is my son's birthday and I have promised him a view." The soldiers parted.

I tried to hide my eyes. "No, Father!"

"You have nothing to fear. These people die because God has made it so. We are here to do God's bidding. God does not want a son of mine to feel fear."

"Father, I do not want to see!" I struggled against his grip, turned my head, and shut my eyes.

"You will see!" He smacked my face with his hand. "Do not shame your father!"

One of the guards laughed.

"Who laughed?" asked Father. The men were silent. All I heard were the cries of the prisoners. "Stop!" ordered Father as he nearly dragged me into the center of the line. "You guard." He pointed to a gangly man.

"Not I, sir." The guard kept his eyes down and his head low.

"Do you call me a liar?"

"No, sir."

Then the man stepped up to my father.

"Son, pick out one of these prisoners. Today, you will have the power to save one of these wretched lives. Now walk along the line and pick out the one you will save."

All my Father's men and the prisoners looked at me. I breathed deeply and raised my head. Father loosened his grip and then let me free.

I inspected the line. A tall man with a long curled ivory beard stood in front and pleaded with me; I wide-stepped around him. A dark-skinned man shook with tears rolling down his face. He spoke in a language I did not understand. I went farther, keeping my distance but looking at each. So many prisoners—I followed the line until I grew tired.

A man in shepherd's clothing stood tall with wide shoulders and skin faded by the sun, the wind, and the rain. He had wisdom about him, a silent strength, not said by words but by his eyes. Yes, his eyes; they were deep like a falcon's but did not weep. "Save the woman behind me."

I paced up to him.

He stood erect and inspected me until my eyes dropped. I swear he smiled at me. Something hung around his neck—a medallion on a chain with a ram deeply stamped into it. It appeared ancient...maybe Roman?

"Would you like this?" He managed to pull it from his neck and offered it in my direction. I stepped closer. Yes, an ancient Roman coin. Mama had once shown me similar artifacts. "It can be yours. Save the woman behind me."

Father caught up behind me and humphed. Hot breath tunneled over the top of my head. "Do not tempt my son with a bribe. He is not so weak."

"I have chosen. The woman, Father, save the woman." I pointed to her as she huddled and shivered behind the man who had offered me the coin.

My father nodded and beckoned the soldier accused of laughing at me towards him. "Off with your armor. You will take the woman's place in line." Then his voice rose to a fierce level. "Let this be a lesson to all! What is your name?" Father asked the guard who was now nearly naked.

"Ion, sir." The man lowered his head, his eyes downward and his hands clutched in prayer.

"Ion will die a brave and honorable death. Spare him no pain. None of my soldiers feel pain. Listen. You will not hear him cry out. He is not weak like these Turks and thieves! He is one of Dracula's men." Then Father patted him on the back. "No man will laugh at my son."

The rest of the guards bowed their heads low.

"Now, for the woman." Father went to her and lifted her chin. "She is a pretty wench." Then he glanced at her belly. "But, son, I said you must pick only one. Do not think you can fool your father by saving two lives instead." He looked down at me. "Choose–the baby or the woman."

My tears formed but did not fall from my eyes. I looked away. I inhaled. Every bit of me shuddered from inside to out and barely could I stand. "The woman, Father...the woman."

The man with the medallion turned and tried to free himself from his ropes.

"No! No! No!" The woman screamed as several guards grabbed her arms and pulled her from the line. Her hair was a mix of sweat and straw. I guessed from last night's bed. She struggled and spat out angry tears with words I could not understand.

I heard the sound of my father's sword as it slid from its sheath. I could not watch but saw from my eye's corner. A rapid thrust and the woman screamed with pain. Father had killed the baby within her!

"Now you can go." Father's hand motioned off towards the hills. He wiped his sword clean and put it back in its sheath.

She stumbled two or three steps and fell to the ground. Her hands tried to keep her insides from falling out. Her body shook, and she rolled on the ground in a puddle of blood. Maybe it was a better way to die?

I vomited again. The rhythm of my pained heaves mixed with the spittle laughter bursting from my father. "Oh, Son, your stomach will grow stronger with each death you see. It is not so bad."

Then he made me watch the most horrible sight ever. The lines of naked prisoners filed one by one up to the horses. A pile of long poles stacked to one side. A man rubbed pig fat and oil on the poles as they sat in a large stack.

One by one, the prisoners struggled against the guards which forced them into place. Some cried and others pleaded. Loops of rope hung at the horses' sides and these were wound tight to each limb of the poor captives. The horses side-stepped and widened their distance between each other. Then the prisoner stretched and hung mid-air. I could not believe the sight! Two of the largest guards lifted a pole from a nearby pile. They balanced it at the prisoner's backside. Then, like a chicken about to be roasted, they slid the stick up through their entire body. The impaled cried out in agony. When the pole came out of their mouth or sometimes shoulder, they silenced. Then the men hoisted the body up, dropped the pole in a hole, Leaving the dying twisting in pain, and moved on to the next. It was as though they planted a garden of men.

It sickened me. My mind raced and could not believe what it saw. I wished I had never ventured outside of the castle gate—ever! I vomited twice more until I could vomit no more.

The guard Father picked made only a little noise. He grunted and sighed as the pole slid slide through his body. Those who watched cheered and crossed themselves in his honor.

I noted the man with the medallion. They pulled his body wide and the pole thrust through him. He did not cry out. I swear—he did not cry out!

***

It was late and all was dark. As though trudging through heavy mud, I made my way to my chambers—my feet like anvils and my mind numb. The wooden sword with my name carved into the shaft lay centered on my bed; I threw it against the wall. What did I care about swords?! The unending sobs and tears filled my bed cover. I did not sleep. People were on poles outside of the castle walls! I looked at the ceiling as I tried to control my breath. If I closed my eyes, they were still there twisted and naked as they died. Their spirits were slow to leave their bodies. Always they reminded me of the frogs. Bulged eyes, mouths opened, and gasping for air, they made strange noises. They were frogs. Somehow, in my mind I repeated—everything is fine. They are frogs. Winding and turning, they gurgled and hopped with big eyes for a silent retreat to Heaven.

CHAPTER 2

Frog Dreams

The night is still. I toss a rock down into the ravine and hear it pop, pop, pop, on the way down. Remembering causes me to shiver—or is it the cold? I sigh lying back on the rock and seeing a shooting star with a bright burning tail swim across the sky. It wiggles like a tadpole and I remember the frogs again.

I hated frogs. Terrible dreams haunted me after my birthday. The frogs invaded my peace almost every night. They talked to me, sometimes. They cried, sometimes. They always grabbed me with their wet sticky fingers and sucked me out of any sleep I might have had. They ate dinner, sometimes. They played. Always they looked at me with those silent, dark round eyes that shone like wet pebbles. Those eyes drove me to madness! I found my reflection in their eyes. I was myself, sometimes. I was my father, sometimes. I turned into a frog and I started to gurgle as I died—many times. Oh, it frightened me!

My mother was frightened too. She often came to my bedside and shook me from my slumber. "Mihnea, wake up. Wake up, son or the devil may grab your soul!" She pulled the sweat-soaked hair from my eyes with, "tell me son about your dreams."

I spoke of the frogs, always. She knew why I dreamt these things. She knew I had seen the horrible deaths, but she never spoke of them. It was in her eyes—dark reflections like when I leaned over into the deep well and looked down. When father was gone on one of his ill-defined affairs, she slept by my side. She told the chamber guards and her ladies, "If you tell my husband, I'll slit your throat myself." She gripped my hand. "Everything is well." She kissed my forehead with, "Sleep like a lamb. Do not worry. Sleep, my child." And I did.

***

I sigh, touching her comfort again. It was the love of my mother that carried me through such darkness. It is not the only memory of my true mother, but it is the fondest. Without her, I may not have survived. Mama Tudora is as strong but in different ways. The women in my life have been a blessing. Then I let my memories float ahead in time.

My favorite play was with the sword. On some mornings, I commanded the stable boys to fight against me with sticks. I believed my skills were better than theirs, but in hindsight, they may have let me beat them. One of these mornings, a servant approached. "Young Master Mihnea, your father requests your audience at the front gate," he said.

I nodded in response and slid my sword into my belt. Why me? Why would Father need me? Hardly had he spoken a word since my birthday. Scattered thoughts—my mind's eye matched the maze of stone wall passages as I hurried to the front gate. Father and Sir Stefan stood together in conversation. I approached and nodded as silently as a sparrow in flight.

"Is he ready?" Father looked down at me. Sir Stephan paced around me in his guard uniform. He stroked his double chin as he scrutinized me up and down. Though he was a large man with a round belly, he moved soft-toed like a cat about to jump on a bird. "Arms up and out," Sir Stephan instructed me.

I did as Sir Stephan commanded. I held the position so long almost like I was acting out the crucifixion. My arms began to shake, as he prodded me on my shoulders. Will I become the newest gate guard? No, that couldn't be.

"He hasn't much strength," stated Sir Stephan. Father nodded in agreement. "His height and reach are average." Father nodded again only this time looking disappointed. "Mihnea, follow this with your eyes." Sir Stephan held a glove and moved it up and down, side to side, and all about. I felt like a horse under the inspection of the stable folk for a sale. Sir Stephan stepped away as though in deep thought. "I can train him."

Train me? The sword! But, of course! Father was asking for my formal training.

"Sir Stephan, I appoint you to teach my son well in the use of the sword," Father said.

"Yes. As it is yours and God's wish, I will train Mihnea."

I felt as though I could burst! I would be trained in sword fighting by the best of our guards. Standing tall, I contained my emotions. Father left and I continued to keep still.

"Meet me in the courtyard tomorrow before the cock crows," Sir Stephan said as he relaxed, I think from Father's exit and smiled. "Bring your sword."

Sir Stefan worked with me in the castle courtyard, every morning and night. Though his body showed signs of too much food and wine, he moved swiftly with his sword and expected the same from me. "Do not move away from me! Step into my thrust." Sir Stefan demonstrated the move.

Sometimes Sir Stefan would show up dressed as a foreigner. Once, he had dressed like the Sultan himself. Covered in fine fabric, he used a Turk's sword to fight me. I laughed so much! "Do you laugh at me?" The boom of his voice made his belly jiggle. "Do I not bring fear into your heart?"

Father would sometimes watch from a window above. He never laughed out loud, but I would catch his smile from time to time. He had in mind some plan, but what, I did not know.

When we practiced, it was always like play to me. Sir Stefan and I would stop because we were laughing so hard. But as we continued practice became more serious. I suspect the growing intensity was Father's suggestion.

I grew some little ways and felt I was getting stronger. I tired easily at first; especially after a sleepless night. I ignored my weariness and more and more enjoyed the swing of my sword.

At first, I used my wooden sword. It was oiled slick and through time Sir Stefan had new wood swords created by the castle carpenters; the size and weight of the swords grew along with me. I think he had in mind to help my strength grow. Then on my thirteenth birthday, without fanfare, I was given a real sword. True, it was smaller in size than the soldiers, but it felt good to hear the metal clang as I fought off Sir Stefan.

Sometimes, he would become winded and sit on one of the garden benches on the courtyard side. "Mihnea, you are improving." He took a deep breath and rested during one of our sessions. For a moment, we sat silent. Then he studied me. "I do not have a son of my own." He turned up to the sky as a hawk flew overhead. "If I did, I would want him to be like you. It is true, I think you are a good son."

I was uncertain why the words meant so much to me. I sat quietly for a moment. I thought about my father, whose time was always elsewhere and not with me or my mother. His grin was infectious and I nodded smiling with a "Thank you."

"I look forward to fighting alongside you when the time comes." He grinned and patted me on the knee.

"And, I you." I brushed some dust off my pants. "Sir Stefan. I think though to keep you swift, I may make you go on a special diet."

"No, please, Young Master. I will stand in front of you and fight off the Sultan's men. Even take a sword's wound. But, do not take my food and wine!"

I laughed. "As long as you can keep moving quickly and not get winded, I will not speak to the kitchen cooks."

He nodded with a smile. "Oh, thank you, Young Master!"

One night shortly after I had earned a true sword, Mama came to see me to bed. Father was off again on some more important task.

"Mihnea, how do you fare tonight?"

I wanted her to know I was less and less of a boy. I took a breath and thought about what my father might say. At the age of thirteen, I was approaching manhood. "Woman, I do not need your visits!" I yelled out, "Go!"

She looked straight at me with pooled tears in the low of her eyes. "I see. Young Master, sleep well." Then she left and I regretted my words. It was her last visit to my chamber. As night pulled me into dark turmoil, the frog dreams came again. Their bodies twitched and one with the same small pools of my mother's eyes croaked out "Why? Why, Mihnea, why?" I woke from the sensation as sweat dripped down my face.

My bed was no longer a place for comfort. It only brought nightmares. The frogs came, always. They looked and acted like people, sometimes. They were as frogs should be, sometimes. It mattered not. I would wake, whenever the frogs came. I started the habit of wandering down to the kitchen.

I ate or drank sometimes, but I would always visit with the kitchen helpers, Voicu and Matei. The boys slept on the floor. I kicked them in the sides until they woke. They did not mind, as they knew I was their Master.

"What now, Master?" Voicu asked as he stretched and got to his feet. "I can cook you something if you wish."

Then Matei would roll, "Oh, it is Young Master. I am sorry. I will be quicker to rise. You do wake me in my best dreams though."

"Is this so bad?" I asked in an angry tone.

"Oh, no, Master. No." Matei jumped up with a forced smile.

"I could not sleep, again. I do not know if my father would approve of my visits. Tell no one. He does not like the poor. But you are both older boys and I am curious about matters which I hope you can tell me about."

"We can only share what we know. It is not much, but we will offer it." Voicu rubbed his hands together in front of the glowing embers in the kitchen fireplace. He turned over the burning log and added another.

"Then I will wake you whenever I sleep not. I will ask questions. I know I am the Master's son, but want to speak with you as friends. I do not want others to know. Do you see?"

"Yes, of course," said Matei.

***

I know I shouldn't have. I know it didn't make sense. I began to think of them as my brothers. The stories were many. I laugh recalling one of my favorites.

***

"I will tell you what I saw only some days ago," said Voicu.

"Tell me, Voicu." I pulled up like a cat looking for a scratch still on my belly. We leaned on our elbows and listened. The stones on the floor were cold and greasy, but I did not mind.

"I left early in the morn. The Mistress appointed me to carry several messages to Arefu. I got up as the rooster crowed and started on my way. I followed the footpath until I heard voices up further in the bend of the river. I skipped along feeling great joy for the warm sunshine and wondering who was out so early. Getting closer, I heard much giggling and splashing. It was a flock of Gypsy women. They swam in the river and bathed without any clothing at all. I was quiet and hid behind a bush. They spoke to each other as Gypsies do, so I knew not what they said. Honestly, I did not care, they were so beautiful!" Voicu said as he held his hand over his heart.

"S'Blood! They were Gypsies!" responded Matei.

We all laughed.

Then I said, "Hush. I do not want to wake anyone." The three of us pulled together closer on the floor.

"I could not take my eyes away. I had never seen a woman without dress," continued Voicu in a whisper. "To me, they were like angels. Then to dry, they went and laid out on a rock in the early morning sun. I cannot tell you how much I wanted to get an even better view. Their skin was smooth and brown. One had breasts big as melons. My heart was pounding so; I forgot my orders. I stepped a little further into the bushes. I did not realize the ground was weak and, as it broke away, I slide down next to the river edge."

"So did they run?" I asked.

"This is what surprised me. At first, they gasped at my appearance," said Voicu in a hush. "I expected them to run and cover themselves. Instead, they laughed and went about their business. They did not care I saw their nakedness. Gypsies have strange ways."

"What happened next?" asked Matei.

"I blushed and got my senses about me again. I climbed back onto the trail. One yelled in their language and I turned. She made her lips pucker as she spoke something strange to me. The rest of the naked group rolled around on the rock and laughed. So, I dusted off and hurried into town. That is my story."

The nights went like this. I was eager to head down to the kitchen almost as much as I awaited the morning and sword practice. My time with Sir Stephan changed though.

During those days, I was often taken from my sword practice by Father. "Let me have some of this time with my son." He waved Sir Stephan off to the castle gates.

My Father and I, in hurried step, inspected the prisoners. There were many. He liked to torture them. For most, death came over days or sometimes weeks.

"God means for me to take their lives slowly. It is this way," he explained. He shuffled up to a dying man and spoke to him. "Do you see where being a thief gets you? I am only beginning what awaits you after you cross the river. Hell holds no pleasures."

I nodded but kept silent through it all. Death and fear were everywhere my Father took me.

The soldiers and guards rushed to follow my Father's orders. Not doing so would result in receiving the same consequence as the prisoners. Often, it was simple like "Put them on poles," "Cut out their tongues," or "Pull off their skin." My Father's men did not hesitate to follow his requests. If the prisoner was of higher status, he would hold long conversations with them. Sometimes he ate his meals as he became engrossed in their suffering. The guards knew to get a table and chair for him. He would relax as he broke bread and dipped it in a stew. He made me watch too. It was true with my Father, death was everywhere.

"We will fight the Turks together one day," he laughed. "Oh, it will be such fun! You see you have always and will always bathe in death. Death is everywhere. Why be afraid?"

I did not have killing in my mind, but I wanted to fight the Turks. I did not like their looks or their manners. All of their ways angered me. The Knights would tell me stories of when they sword-fought with them. Some Turk fighters were so good they could dislodge two men's heads in one swing of their fancy swords! My blood would boil at the mention of Turks.

Father laughed and clapped as he watched some of the torture. I kept in mind his words- Death is everywhere. When I found myself overtaken by their screams, smells, and vision, I would think of my sword swinging. I would think of stories to share in the coming evening. As my body tensed and my throat tightened, my thoughts finally surrendered to the same path. Only frogs, they are only frogs.

As I grew taller, I noticed the changing ways of the soldiers and guards. They were more careful around me. They did not anger me, laugh at me, or speak to me. They stood still with eyes forward. I wondered if they thought of the days ahead when I would order them. I was uncertain until one day when I overheard some guards as they spoke freely unaware I was around the corner.

"He is like a smaller version of his father." It was true, I had begun to show some of his characteristics—at least in looks. I had the same angular face and long dark curly hair. I had not changed yet. I had no facial hair. The swordplay helped me develop some stringy muscles. In girth, I was very thin but strong; someday, I might grow to be as tall and fierce as my father.

"Do you think he will act the same?"

"Oh, I'd not cross the boy."

Some part of me was so proud. I was becoming powerful. Maybe, I was becoming my father. I jumped from my hiding place and said nothing to the soldiers who stood at attention. It pleased me to circle them and cause them distress. It was power and I began to thirst for it.

Dracula's Son

I was not old enough to go to battle yet. When my father came back from travels and returned with prisoners, he would say, "It will not be so long now, son. Soon, Son, soon."

The wait was over in less than a fortnight. The Turks came to us. Dracula had angered the Sultan enough and he came for revenge. The first words of the war fell on me like thunder. Father rested in his chambers. Voicu hurried up the stairs and down the hall without breathing, as I stepped by with a wink and nod. He smiled nervously at me. I was curious, so I stopped for a moment in front of my chambers. He knocked upon the tall oak boards of Father's door. I heard and felt the vibration of Father's pounding steps as they neared the entrance. Voicu tensed as he waited for it to open.

"Why do you disturb me? I have said never to call me at my chambers unless the Sultan was at my doorstep!" snarled Father.

"Sir." Voicu's voice shook and I saw a puddle of piss form next to his shoe. "One of the scouts from the south arrived with word the Sultan's forces are less than two days away."

Father paced back into his room. Slow with focus, he turned away and picked up his sword. I had seen him do this before to other messengers. Please, not Voicu!

"Sir, what should I do?" asked Voicu as his last words.

I stood down the hall but witnessed it. Father lowered his head in steady silence. He stepped several paces away and then spun. His sword loped off Voicu's head! No! No! No! I steadied myself against the wall. "I said my doorstep! I do not have a door two days away!" The words splattered as violently as Voicu's blood did against the wall. Oh, Voicu is dead. He is gone.

I stood solid as Father searched for my response. He smiled and nodded to me. He sniffed the air. He had known I was watching; of this I was certain. I drained all emotions away as I breathed in. Still. I did not flinch. I did not say a word. Death was everywhere.

CHAPTER 3

The Escape

Petra jumps up startled and alert then hurries off in the brush alongside the canyon edge. The moonlight reflects in the swirl of dark river currents far below. It was a night like this when I first arrived in the mountains. It was the time of the Sultan's attack.

Water droplets gathered on the shoulder of my shirt. The day's mist was a bad sign. I combed my fingers through my dripping hair and stepped over the threshold of the Great Hall.

Father assembled his chief warriors. They gathered at the long table in anticipation of his orders. He stood at the front of the Great Hall appearing more like a statue than a man—massive and proud. The wind whistled over the rafters above. The men's eyes glassily reflected the shine of Father's armor.

"We will not go to meet them. This is what they want," he stated calmly. Father did not acknowledge his men's presence in words or actions. He picked the dirt out from under his fingernails. It appeared casual as if he were in preparation for evening prayer. "We live in a fortress. We will defend our home and the Turks will be forced into our game. I want to hear from you. Speak up!" He slammed the tabletop with his palm.

The silence was a special kind much like a hunter pursuing prey. I breathed out feeling my tongue press against my teeth and I swallowed the gathering spit. Father slithered around close behind each of his men. I admired his power. My neck hairs stood as straight as the castle's front guards in anticipation of his next action.

"If you do not speak upon these matters, then I will find someone who will. I have assembled you to have your advice and counsel. Do not be worms with me. Be men!"

Feet shuffled under the table and then a voice. It was one of the oldest warriors, Sir Mathew by name. "Sir, could we send a legion to draw away some of their power? It would not cost us so much and we could still defend the castle."

Father kept his pace, marching around the table. He stopped behind Sir Mathew. The sound of a good blade being pulled from its' place left no questions in the warriors' minds. Father set the tip of the sword on Sir Mathew's neck. "Defend yourself."

"Sir, I am here to do your bidding."

"Then I ask you again to defend yourself."

"Sir, I cannot…" his words were cut short and the sharp blade severed his head. It rolled out into the table's center. The men shuffled uncomfortably. Father now had their full attention. Glances connected. Some steadied their scared and war-torn hands upon the oak table top.

Father continued to circle the table and smiled as he soaked in his power. His pace did not change so close to each his garb brushed against the backs of their chairs. He scanned the room with shifting eyes seeking a dagger to come out from under the table. Would one of them jump up in challenge? I felt my chest pump and I did not blink fearing I would lose sight of some action.

"Who is with me?" Father snarled through his teeth. The men sat in silence. Another head came off and fell to the floor. "I asked who is with me."

A mixture of "I am" and "We are" floated around the room.

"Who do you fear more, gentlemen, the Sultan or me?"

"You, sir" and "Without a doubt, you, sir" and just plain "You" bounced over the table.

My father continued his march around the table. "Good," he said. "If I am not a feared leader, then I am a weak leader. I will ask you again. Tell me your thoughts on these matters."

Then a young warrior I did not know pushed away from the table and stood up. "Sir, I am at your service. Tell me what to defend and I will defend it."

"Good! I will send you and your men out to welcome the Sultan. I suspect none of you will live. Do you fear death?"

"No, sir." He kept his glance downward.

"Then you may leave the table. You will prepare your men for war."

The warrior bowed his head and all others nodded in his direction as he trotted out the main door.

The discussion of the coming battle continued throughout the day. Father did not sit. He continued his steady pace around the table. I kept tall with folded arms and leaned against the cold stone wall. The discussion between Father and his men steadied, though his sword never left his hand. His steps made the floorboards creak and bend under his weight. I wondered if ever I would be so powerful. My mind wandered to daydreams of battle with mad Turks as I peeked out the nearest window.

I became hungry and bored, so I wandered to the kitchen. I nodded to Matei as I neared the pantry. He turned away with red swollen eyes. I realized news of Voicu's fate must have reached him. He hurried by and did not acknowledge my presence. I thought he was weak but had some slight ache in my heart knowing I too would miss Voicu. He was a friend.

I heard Father's angered voice echo across the courtyard. I hopped from stepping stone to stepping stone. Then I scuffed softly back into the Great Hall. My stomach was full of sausage and buttered rolls. I noted two more heads had been displaced. One lay on the floor with the headless body slumped against the nearest man. The other sat on the tabletop next to Sir Mathew's. I laughed thinking the two heads appeared as though they were in conversation. I lifted a half-full glass of mead excitedly and anticipated the coming battle. Finally, I would be able to use my sword. I imagined smashing the Turks. Oh, how I hated them! When I pictured them, it was as though a spark lit deep inside of me. Quick shots flamed out seeking to burn the demons.

"Son, come over here."

I pranced up to my Father's side. I was still a hog's head below his stance but knew he meant for me to stand tall. He pulled me close as he put his arm around my shoulders and all eyes were on me.

"Are you a man?"

"Not yet, Father."

"No, I didn't think so." Blood dripped from his face. He grinned, then he shoved me away from full force and I fell on one warrior's body which slept eternally upon the floor.

I pushed myself up from the corpse. I took deep slow breaths of blood vapors and bile reminding myself death is everywhere. I inspected the severed head swimming in a mix of dark and bright red pools. I stood, suddenly tired, and noted blood that wasn't mine candle-waxed down the front of my shirt.

"We will not have our women and children fighting this battle." Father's voice was calm and clear. "The castle is for their protection. You and your men will make battle beyond the safety of the castle. I will have a select group to command from my keep. Do we all understand?"

"Yes, sir." All nodded.

"Then, I bid you leave."

The men marched out. They appeared fierce and bloodied by battle already. Father intended this look for effect, no doubt. They were to go directly to their men and give orders. Stopping by the horse troth for a wash was not possible.

A servant ran in and bowed to my father as she offered him a bowl of water. He dipped his hands in. Her eyes cast downward, and he slapped her. "Lazy women, get this mess cleaned!" She bowed again and nearly touched the floor. Then she hurried about trying to match heads with bodies. Father placed the water bowl on the table and nodded to me. I dipped my hands in the bloodied water. Father exited in silence.

I stepped into the hall and watched the guards assist the servants as they carried out bodies and heads. I had admitted I wasn't a man yet. I kicked the wall. When I was fully grown, how would I be? Strong? Weak? Powerful? Would I be a leader? Would I be famous? Would I bring fear into men's hearts?

***

Now I am a man. My greatest weakness is found in a lie. Petra returns wagging his body and settling alongside me. I scratch behind his ears. "What should I do Petra? How can I tell my family, my love, that I have been living a lie?" Deer silently trek along a path below. They are quietly grazing. They do not know I am watching. Silent and dark, under the stars, the air turns cool and I pull my cape on to keep some warmth and energy as I retrace the steps of my past.

***

I had no fear. Who were these foreigners to come and try to threaten our homeland? I went to find one of the Knights to practice my sword.

"Is Sir Stefan here?" I asked the guards at the front gate.

"He is with your father. None of us may practice with you today. We must prepare for battle."

The Turk prisoners, maybe several hundred, were being impaled as I exited the gate; I made little note of this. I hated them and felt they were getting what they deserved. Won't it be a pretty sight for the Sultan and his forces! Maybe, I had become my father.

I hiked the fields outside smelling the reek of death mixed with distant screams. The water in the river below was flowing fiercely and I became lost in thought. How will this battle look? Would we soon have the Sultan's head up on a golden pole for all to view? I laughed at the thought and noted the pale blue sky as a raven flapped in a wounded fashion overhead. Then I heard Mama's voice from behind.

"Son, come near!" She shadowed me on the path. The gate guards must have told her where I ventured. "You should not be out here."

I stopped as she hurried closer. Mama shone with confident beauty in her flowing dress with hair tied sideward. For the first time in so very long, she took my hand. "Come with me to the tower wall. We can look down to see all."

We had heard stories of the Sultan's weak past efforts and laughed as we swung our hands between us. I grinned keeping her soft grip. I had so missed Mama. I followed behind as we climbed the narrow spiraling stairs. Up, up, up!

"We can watch the Sultan give up his men from here," Mama pushed the guard aside and we climbed to the top. Mother held her arms wide causing the wind to billow her sleeves which forced her to step back from the wall. We smiled as though some great play was being presented for our viewing below.

I squinted noting several soldiers rode quickly on horseback through the front gate. They moved in silence, so far below. Later, I would hear the two men lose their heads as they delivered the message to my father. The Sultan's forces were fully three times the size of Father's! Still, Father's army was better trained. One of our men could overtake a dozen of theirs.

"Mihnea do not underestimate The Sultan. He is like your father a powerful man. I want you to know that, whatever the outcome of this battle, my love for you will never end. Someday, when you are in power, I hope you will make the right choice. There are powers greater in this world than fear," Mama looked at me. I nodded in silent agreement.

Later, I hurried with my sword to practice in the courtyard. Back and forth my sword swooshed! I pictured Turk heads falling across the ground. I laughed.

Mama stayed in her quarter's the rest of the day. I thought she must be praying.

Night came. I turned in my bed and squinted toward the candle, as the icon of the Virgin Mary looked to dance from the flicker. Tired of excitement, I fell into a deep and satisfying sleep.

***

Father stood in the courtyard near the Great Hall as I sought early morning word. "Today, Son, the battle begins. I want you to watch over your Mama. Protect her. Keep harm away."

"Yes, Father. I will protect Mama." He squeezed my shoulder with, "Good. I will depend on you." He strode off pointing in this direction and then another as he spoke to his men.

I made my way to the front gate, with a quick step. It closed tight. Some of the women were shouting at the guards. "No one may leave. These are our orders. Do you want to bring it up with Dracula?" The ladies scuttled away and reminded me of chickens that scratched in the dirt for bugs. I could see one shake as she cried on another's shoulder. Oh, women!

I went to check on Mama. I wondered if she was concerned like the other women. I would ease her burdens. I could comfort her. Her chamber door closed, which was unusual for the time of day. I knocked. "Mama, it's me."

"Oh, Mihnea, come in."

The light was grey inside and the air was still. Mama sat on her bed as she gazed out the window. Her hair was uncombed and her dress unfit. She did not look like the lady of the castle. "Why are you so?" I asked as the volume of my voice rose. Then I could see some bags under her eyes. "Did you not sleep?"

"No, Son." She took my fingers and petted them.

I pulled my hand away and raised my voice in anger. "My lady, can you not find your place? How can the rest of the women feel any safety, if you are so?"

She lifted her eyes to me without any words. She was tense and the corners of her mouth twitched as though suppressing some deep emotion. I exited without another word. I stepped out the main door shaking my head and feeling humored by her fear.

Later, I would understand Mama's concerns. The Turks were already setting up their cherry wood canons on the bluffs of Poenari. A line of them appeared across the river and with a full view of the castle. The numbers were uncountable. Those going into battle renamed the plains across the river The Field of Cannon and this was fitting.

I recalled all I knew of castle sieges. They could go on for months or years. I expect Father thought this campaign would last for an extended time. Still, he prepared for full battle.

The Turks began to send shots toward the castle. The caliber of the firearm was too weak. Our castle would not be taken by some distant cannons. Many of the shots fell harmlessly into the river below. Others bounced off the rock walls-having little effect.

Father stayed at the table in the Great Hall. He paced sometimes and other times sat quietly. I peeked in but did not disturb.

I overhead, as one of the men reported, "They have little compared to our forces, but their numbers are growing. The rest of the Sultan's armies are on the move and soon will crowd the hills and valleys of the area."

"As I expected." Father kept calm and held his anger. Deep furrows showed on his forehead. I became tired as I sat on the bench outside, so I went up to the tower wall. The guards stopped me at the top.

"Young Mihnea, you must stay below. The Master ordered us to allow no one up here." A guard I had never seen before blocked my entry.

I lied. "My father has given me orders to look from here and report the standings. Do you object?"

"No, of course not. Take care though, as some of the broken rock does fly high."

I stepped out and scanned over the wall. Dizzy. The river far below appeared active with ants. A closer inspection defined them as men of my father's army. They ran from here to there. Some shouted orders, and others moved in mass.

"Where are the Turks?"

"Look to the bluff, Young Master. See the smoke?"

And then I did. Hundreds of soft lines of campfire smoke rose to the sky like ropes tied to the clouds. I suspected a hundred men for each fire. Oh, so many Turks!

The sun was beginning to set and I, in the chill of the air, decided to check on Mama. I stepped down the spiral of stairs and hurried down the hall to the Master Chambers.

I knocked. "Mama, are you okay?"

She opened the door and her presence radiated out into the hall. "Enter, my son."

She was once again the lady of the castle. The royal shimmer of a red velvet dress glowed from her. Her hair was braided cleanly and showed off the shine of her strands. Her maids bowed to us as they exited. Her eyes were sharp and her smile sincere. "I hope my looks please you."

"Yes, Mama, you look as you should."

She laughed. But in the laugh, I read something. It was formal and stiff; the wall around her true emotions higher than any castle holds. I had wanted a battle, but I had not pictured Mama in it also.

"Now, I must go speak well to the women. You were right, Son. I need to present some calm," she said.

And so she pranced out to be seen in public. I strolled on to the next door down the hall—my chambers. I went in and found a fresh bowl of water to wash my face. I did not know it, but this would be the last time I would spend in the comfort of my room.

I wandered the castle as the grey sky turned black. Some Rock Doves flew overhead bringing the smell of battle with them. I sat on a bench in the courtyard silently wishing I could sneak off and slit the Sultan's throat. How dare he cause such a disruption! He will pay!

***

I throw another stone down the gully and scare up some birds sleeping on the branch of a tree down below. "Caw! Caw!" and flap, flap, flap. Though I have many hard memories, this is the hardest. I remember Mama's death.

Dusk came like a chant before a funeral. I spotted Mama stepping into her chambers. She lit a candle and then closed the door. The air was still but held a kind of energy—the kind one feels the instance before a wolf pounces from the forest.

In the courtyard, I reclined on a stone bench listening. There was commotion throughout the castle and battle sounds muffled beyond.

Above, an ancient man yelled. Some of the cook's little children wandered by and waved. I waved back. So much went on as it always did.

Then Father rushed by. "This is no time to longue." He slapped me hard with the back of his hand. My face stung. "Go help brush down the horses. I will not have a son of mine relaxing while we are at battle! You will meet me at my chambers when you are finished."

"Yes, Father." I limped away avoiding the full light. In the dark of the hall, I rubbed off the tears from my eyes. I smelled sweet manure which somehow comforted me, as I approached the castle stables. A Stable Hand passed me a brush in the dim light of the overhead torch. "Master said you would be coming."

I sauntered by the Ferrier who was busy in the glow shoeing some of the horses. I stopped at the curious sight. The strong stench of sweat was everywhere as he acknowledged my presence with a grunt. I raised my eyebrows, noting he had placed the shoe upside down on the horses' feet. "Under orders" with huffing breath he smiled.

One of the stable hands directed me to a clean paddock where a horse awaited my brush. I placed one hand upon the solid neck-muscled brown velvet fur. Then, I brushed back and combed out the burrs of the chestnut's last run. I got lost in the scent of the stables.

"Young Mihnea." A guard approached as the horse stepped away from my hand and brush. "Your Father summons you to his chambers."

I hopped up the stairways two steps at a time to the Master Chambers. Familiar voices rose—Mama and Father. The shouting carried through the thick walls as the two sounded as though in battle themselves. I did not enter but looked in as Mama handed Father something. "It is a note which came from the arrow shot into our chamber from one who still follows you. The Sultan attacks at daylight with full force. He will overtake the castle!" She was in tears. Her hair hung everywhere.

Father must have heard my step as he glanced into the hall. "Son, go fetch me a courier. Now!"

I ran down the steps as I sensed the urgency. Something was wrong and did not fit my father's plans. I found a courier below and urged him to haste to my parent's chambers. I followed behind, finding it difficult to keep up with the man's step.

"I would rather my body be eaten by the fish of the Arges than to be a Turk's slave!" Mama shouted as she ran by and with tears set her eyes upon me for the last time. Down the hall and up the stairs to the tower wall, she rushed.

Father came out. "Take this to the Lords of Arefu. Do not get captured." The messenger nodded as he took the scroll.

"Where is your mother?" I turned to the tower stairs. Father threw me to the floor.

He ran the full flight of stairs up to the tower and then I heard an unearthly howl! Did Mama jump? I imagined her body down below—bent and twisted among the boulders as the river roared. How can this be? There was another set of screams as Father threw the guards over the wall. Down the stairs, he stumbled. I sobbed as he grabbed me so hard I thought my chest would burst open. "Did I not tell you to care for your Mama?" He slapped me with such force; I heard a snap in my head. I fell against the wall spitting blood and snot. He covered his eyes and screamed all the way. Down into the Great Hall, he ran and slammed the main door so hard it seemed to shake the whole castle.

I sat on the floor and wept. Alone. Mama gone. I could not imagine such a world. Mama dead. Then I closed my eyes and what image blurred into existence? Her red dress appeared like the head of a giant reddened mushroom. She floated through the air…then her feet began to enlarge and web as her eyes grew big. I saw Mama as a frog. She was swimming and gulping her way down the river. The eyes are what drove me mad! They penetrated me saying, Why, Son, why did you not take care of me? I punched my fists against the wall until they were raw and bloodied. I felt numb. Angry at myself. Death is everywhere, Son. Death is everywhere. I curled against the wall and pulled my knees in tight. I heard no noise except my uncontrolled sobs and sucking breaths. This was my safety—my new womb.

"Begging your pardon, Young Master." Matei approached me. I thought of my tears and how I must appear as he did earlier—red-eyed with sadness. "I was sent for you. Your father has messengers out for assistance. He asked me to bring you Voicu's clothes. I do not know why. A meeting will take place in the Great Hall. You must attend." He extended his hand, pulled me up, and brushed off my back. I put my hand on his shoulder and he put his on mine. We stood for a moment glancing into each other's souls and remembering we were brothers. I nodded and followed behind him.

Two guards, a dozen men, Sir Stefan and Father were in the hall. Noise from our gunnery and shots from the distance flavored the air. From the sounds, I guessed the battle would take full force in the morning light.

Father had sent for help from the village as they owed him their allegiance. Two men in travel clothes entered.

"Secure the door." The guards followed Father's orders. He appeared composed but tired. "I will not be outwitted by the Sultan! He has a large army—well stocked and prepared. He thinks he has conquered me. He does not know I have been planning this escape from a time well before my castle was constructed. My plan kept silent, as all the builders died before the final stone was set. I alone know this secret." What was he talking about?

The small group kept silent at the table. I did not know what to think. We were trapped in the Great Hall. Once the Sultan takes the castle, he will burn us inside. The scene was hopeless.

Then Father leaned forward with a raging grin, "The Sultan can have my castle, but he will not have me!" He held a fist in the air. "Stand up all of you. Stand back! Move the table and chairs to the side." The men did not question his order. He pointed to the rug. "Remove it."

I rubbed my eyes thinking they deceived me for below the rug sat an ancient door with a rusted pull. Some gasped. One of the village men clapped and laughed.

"You are my most faithful servants. I return the favor by saving your lives." He nodded around the room. "This door opens to a passage. Long and winding, it will take us to a cave someway down the river." Father's eyes were wide and excited. "Before the Sultan's men could capture the riverside, I had the Ferrier shod horses backward. This is to confuse the Turks. Some of my best men snuck these down to a well-hidden cave and await us. "Over these past years, I have been in constant contact with the King of Hungary. He waits presently with troops beyond Brasov. He will meet us with great protection.

"I have asked the Lords of Arefu to provide us with the best guides. These men have just arrived. They will help us to find passage over the Fargaras Mountains." The two men nodded in assurance. "We will have to move quickly. My son and I must prepare for the journey. If we are captured no one must know who we are."

I followed my father's lead as he began to undress. We were assisted, as we put on servant clothing. I noticed Voicu's shirt was still stained with his blood; he would not have died in vain. Father took a sharp blade and looked at his reflection in a shield. He shaved off his mustache and transformed into someone I had never known.

One of the guards grabbed a torch from the wall and bowed to Father. "Shall I go down first?"

Father took the knife and threw it full force at the hall door. Thwack! It stuck solid. "Yes, we will follow you."

I eased cautiously onto the slippery steps. The spiral stairs beyond the cobwebs appeared to disappear into the darkness of hell. I watched the glow as the torch descended. The flame rose and reflected off from slime-coated dripping like candle wax walls. A hand was on my shoulder. I turned to see Sir Stephan. He smiled and prompted me onward.

We wandered in single file down the narrow tunnel and soon the air was thick with the sound of—drip, drip, drip. It was dark—too dark to see. Small creatures or demons scampered ahead of us. Did Father tell Mama of this secret? Would she have not jumped, if she knew there was another way to escape the Sultan? I felt my face heat.

I heard a splash and the guard leading shared, "I'm at the bottom." He waded ahead torch in hand through what sounded like deep water. My eyes adjusted. A bat fluttered by and I flinched.

"Quick now, we haven't time to waste!" Father spat out in an echoed voice.

Through the water, we waded. I slipped on the rocks. Seeking footing, again and again, I submerged under the icy waters. Sir Stephan pulled me up as I gulped, sputtered, and coughed out water. "Hurry, Young Master!" he said.

Father's silhouette moved far ahead.

I felt lifted as Sir Stephan carried me above the water. He stepped on strong and forceful. He set me upon the rocky shore of this underground waterway. I hurried ahead on my hands and knees through a shallow tunnel. I worried for a moment Sir Stephan might not fit, but a prod from behind let me know otherwise.

I grappled along trying to catch the light ahead. I breathed full with my belly wide and my heart pounded like the drum of battle. I pulled along until my arms shook from aching. Finally, the tunnel widened and opened into a vast cave. I do know how long we had crawled, but the strain left me weary.

Brushing the heavy mud from my hands and knees, I turned back to see each man of the company as they wiggled from the hole. It was as though the earth gave birth to men.

"The horses are ahead." Father's voice was in a jagged whisper.

We were quiet and still for some time. I could hear the Turk's camp not far to the north. They sang and sounded as if in celebration. What would they do if they found us? My breath sounded heavy and I covered my mouth with trembling hands.

Ahead in the bushes, I heard a whinny and hooves kicked up dirt—the horses. Each in our group took a mount and the waiting soldiers let go of the reins, bowed low to Father, and ran off into the dark.

"You will ride with me, Son." Father plucked me up like a sack of grain and dropped me near the beast's rump. "Men, we must hurry through the mountains. Fresh mounts await us along the way." We took off into the solid dark at a full gallop the instant I gripped Father's tunic.

We rode on without stopping to increase our distance from the Turks. Father spoke to me on such matters. "If they catch you, do not tell them who you are. Trust has killed many. No one must know who you are until we are safe with the army in Hungary. Do you hear my words?"

"Yes, Father. I will not speak of who I am until we are in Hungary." The steam from horse breath rose into what I was certain would soon turn into the morning mist. I wished for food, rest, for comfort, but there was none.

And so we rode without stop—through the woods, up hills, through stony crags, and down hills. We rode the full day stopping only once to change mount and relieve ourselves. Oh, my bottom was sore! Even my hands numbed as I gripped tight to Father's shirt. I wanted to rest but knew it would cause anger. And, so, I held on. We continued into the dusk and evening. My head fell forward until I could stand it no longer, "Father, I'm tired."

We were in full darkness, but he found the means to slap my face. Shocked, I fell from the horse and rolled into darkness. He shouted from his hurried steed, "I cannot be slowed! A new bitch will bear better pups!" I meant nothing to him. He could live with my death but not the burden of my company. Like a scrap tossed from the table to the hounds, I fell into the dark. Rocks slide under my feet. I reached but found nothing to hold. The ground was gone. I was in the air—and flew! I felt certain the drop would be my death. Gravel splatters far below echoed my target. I hit with a sickening snap! I rolled my head against the hard cold rock and all was dark.

Chapter 4

My New Life

Petra steps up on the sitting rock. I hear his nails drag across the stone as he approaches. "Come here, old dog." The rhythm of scratch, scratch comes closer. He makes an oomph sound as his body drops next to me—his head on my lap. I pat him behind his ears. "Sleep, boy, sleep. You have worked hard today." Then, I remember when I was alone. I woke in the dark. Maybe, it was the same night. Maybe, it was another night.

***

The stars blurred spots through my eyes swollen close to shutting out all light. Gravel slid with even the thought of moving. All I could do was make the smallest of twists and moves. I had felt pain before. The hurt was of a different kind. The sensation was of raw brokenness everywhere. I made the quietest prayers—my hands and arms too much in pain to come together. My father had left me to die. Mama was dead. Death was everywhere. I closed my fluttering eyelids.

The black of the night did not allow me to assess my condition. I suffered as I have never suffered. Breathing happened, but with such pain. My chest was heavy as though a sack of oats sat upon it. I focused all my effort on the air coming in and going out. It helped me some.

And this is how I spent two days…maybe more. When the light came, I could twist to the side and find my legs as I squinted down the slope.

They sat at a funny angle, both bloodied and swollen. With time, I realized most of my aches were from this part of my body.

With complete focus, I moved my arms. I flexed my fingers in curls and felt less pain when I concentrated on them. Father had left me to die. To him, I was nothing but a burden slowing the pace. Through all my pain, my thoughts tortured me the most. I understood my father and myself better as I suffered alone close to death. He called Mama a bitch—and just as she neared the gates of heaven! This I would never forgive. His efforts had caused me to distance Mama. He had tossed me to die. I was full of hatred for him. Should I go to hell for such thoughts, I will tell the demons I fear them not as my father is eviler than all of them combined.

A piece of me hoped the Turks had captured him. Maybe they would torture him as he had done to so many. I pictured him high on a pole. It was with these thoughts I knew I could see my father as only one thing—evil. To leave me to die was unforgivable. I did not ever care to be with him again. Yet, he was my only family. I was ready to die. If I should go to heaven, I would be with Mama.

Mixed with my anger and pain, I was certain death would come soon. I was glad to be dying in the mountains. I closed my eyes and focused as I heard the birds singing and flying overhead. I also, now and then, heard a scamper of a squirrel or some other rodent down below. They were invisible. But I saw the birds. Oh, how I wanted to fly.

The birds darted in low scatters and the sky became cloudy. I heard the crack of thunder, as a storm approached. When the rain began to fall, I realized how parched I was and tried to angle my mouth, so I could catch droplets. It rained and rained and my body began to shake. I could not control it. The shivers brought on more pain. I closed my eyes and prayed God would send an angel soon to take me away.

It was then my body pains subsided. I felt light. It was as though I floated in the river or, no, more like I was floating into the air. Am I dead? At the moment as I floated in comfort, I considered why would anyone fear death?

I was surrounded by darkness but also light. How strange. Yes, there was light and like a moth, to a torch, I was drawn to it. The light was more like pulsing energy. God's blood? And there I was in an open field. In every direction, I was surrounded by people. They were the souls of people I had watched die. I recognized the warriors my father had killed only a day or two ago. They bowed with welcoming smiles as they recognized me. Alongside them was another group- the minstrels; they also smiled in my direction with a deep bow. My soul leaped when I spotted a familiar grin beyond my father's soldiers. It was Voicu! I wanted to reach out to grab my friend's hand but realized somehow I was not allowed to. There were rules here. He spoke but not with his mouth. It was his voice but as though it were my internal voice. You get to select your path forward. I did not understand. Maybe another can help you understand. Communication here in Heaven was so different from on Earth. He moved as though caught in a breeze floating to the side.

I saw a form of light from behind Voicu. First blurred and then becoming clear. She placed her hand on Voicu's shoulder and stepped toward me. Oh, my heart! It was Mama! Son, you must choose- were her words. I still did not understand. She had her eyes upon me. Love. This is one choice-I thought. Her head nodded in agreement. Love.

I looked deep into Mama's eyes. They became whirlpools and I fell in. I floated above the crowd of thousands and thousands. Some I knew. Some I had seen tortured. Some I had seen hoisted up on poles. Voicu and Mama each communicated with me. Pain, torture, and finally the freedom of death. I did not see so much with my eyes as with my heart. One scene after another flashed by. God, have I not had enough pain? But the scenes did not end. And it was not just the people I knew. Many were Turks. I felt confused. They were a part of me. How could I have not known this? But for each, even the Turks, there was this energy. It carried on and I felt other pain- the pains of the still-living. Like drops into a sea, each life had ripples and swirls which shadowed so many lives. I saw mothers who lost sons, wives who lost husbands, and children who lost parents. Neighbors, friends, and endless connections all suffered. Much pain was attached to every single life lost. But what was this about? My father- of course- how did my father keep his power? It was fear. Fear. I must choose love or fear.

I floated back to my position looking back at Mama. She nodded smiling. Love or fear- I must choose my path. Then a bright light appeared behind Mama. I must go. I leave you with the greatest gift I have- my love. It is not time for you yet. I will wait until we will meet again. Who was behind Mama? I could not imagine. She faded and like mist soon disappeared. He stood tall and strong- it was the man with Falcon's eyes. The man from the line on my long-ago birthday. In his hand was the necklace made with an old Roman coin. Please, take this. It shone in a way I hadn't noticed the last time he offered it. Take this. I knew I had made my choice. Love. It is the only thing that matters. Love. I reached for the coin. I stretched and then I felt my body elongate not towards the coin, but back from where I had come. Still, I reached. Back into my body of pain, I was sucked falling like a raindrop from the sky. My hand still searching for the coin. Then something wet touched my palm. It was moist. A tongue. A dog licked my hand. I choose love. An angel did come, but not as I expected. I heard a growl. There were bells and sheep bleating below. Something scampered around the screed circling. It was a dog. "Ruff! A-ruff!"

"We haven't time for you to chase squirrels. Petra, where are you?" said a man's voice.

The dog panted with a wet nose against my face and then another lick. "Hwoof! Hwoof!" the dog shared. Then I heard the sound of a man as he scampered up the rock slide and slope. "Oh, my, a boy! Has he gone to heaven? Could he have survived such a fall?" he asked the dog.

I tried to speak and realized I couldn't. But with an exhale, I groaned.

"Oh, dear, he is alive. We must help him, Petra." The man scrambled up the escarpment. He took off his sheepskin cape and laid it down next to me. "Boy, I need to move you. I am sorry because I know it will pain. Trust me."

Then he rolled me over onto the skin. Ties of sheep-hide strips were wound around tightly. The pain was no better or worse than before. The tight skin did take my chills away. "We must get you to my wife. Petra, watch the sheep." The dog rushed off at the man's signal. Then he slid me down the slope by pulling the skin. My body ached with each bump along the way. I heard the sounds of grassy rhythms and soft raindrops in the breeze as he pulled me along further.

"I have done this with a sheep. I do not think it will be so difficult." He lifted me over his shoulder and carried me. He was strong with long strides and hiked on endlessly. I could not tell how far away his home was, but it was not close. I fell in and out of my senses. Spots of sunlight shone across mushroom and moss-covered passages. In the forest deep, soon droplets of rain gave way to a mist with the strong scent of pine and the bubbling of a stream over rocks. Always, I would wake to find him, my silent carrier, continuing along. My body bounced with each step he took. He did not stop. He did not rest.

A suddenly vibrating volume of "Oh-de! Oh-de! Oh-de! Oh-de!" as he made a mountain call to someone ahead. "Oh-de! Oh-de! Oh-de!" Someone came running towards us.

"What have you?" asked a woman's voice.

"A boy. I will tell all after we have him inside." His strides did not shorten. Then he tilted me downward on a slope and through a doorway. He set me on a side bed. It was warm and sweet smells floated everywhere. I fell into deep darkness. I was uncertain if I was still with breath or in heaven. It must have been some time before I came to my senses. I slept.

"Are you alive, boy?" the woman asked and I opened an eye. I breathed out. With a rag, she wiped my forehead and then squeezed liquid down my throat. "You will be well, but it will take time. Grigore, my husband, found you. Thank God above. Do you have a name boy? I am Tudora. You can call me Mama Tudora."

I rolled to my side and scanned the interiors of the house. It was a home of the poor. The floor was dirt and the walls white. A small fire still smoked from the hearth next to my bed. A loft above was where I suspected they slept. A rough table sat to one side with bowls hung from the wall behind. The room smelled sweet and, then, I saw all the herbs tied in bundles hanging across the rafters. I was warm under several sheepskins.

It was daytime. Light came from small windows above and to each side of the doorway. I reached down with one hand and could feel hardened mud and sticks wrapped around both of my legs. I was in a long shirt of some sort and had no pants.

"Do you need to pee, boy? You must." She grabbed a bowl from the floor and lifted the sheepskin. "I can help," she took my manhood and held the bowl underneath. "There, now. You can pee."

I flushed red to even be in such a state. I peed though it hurt. I had no other option.

"Good boy. Now I need to tend to the lambs outside and I'll dump this. If you should need me, here is a bell you can ring." She scurried away.

I tried to stretch noting the bands of sunlight across the floor. I thought of how lucky I was and about getting better. For the first time I could recall, I realized death was not everywhere. Death was not in this little house. My ears pounded with the movement of my heart—how could he do this to me? As I fell into a deep sweet sleep, I had only one thought—death is not here.

Mama Tudora was an herbalist. She did not stop brewing twigs or leaves and making another tea to go down my throat. It was constant and I felt like the wine bag of a drunkard ever being filled. She stepped quickly around the room and, while she had some grey hair, she seemed youthful. Her hair reminded me of chestnuts but with strands of white everywhere. She was plump. I thought she kept herself to please her husband. I did not know, but my mind tried to better understand these poor people. The way she fussed with washing the clothes and dishes, and all around the house, you'd think she lived in a castle. But most of all, she loved her words. She talked of the day saying, "Oh, it is beautiful outside," or "soon you will be walking," or "I think you may be too thin!" She spoke to me constantly as she hurried about. From time to time, she stopped at my bedside and brush my hair back saying, "Rest, Son, rest."

I remembered Father telling me not to give my true identity until I was in Hungary. I knew for my safety I must continue this. I thought about this some. When I am well, I can sneak away. How would Father react knowing I am still alive? Maybe he would not welcome me, but I hoped someone would. I hated him but who else did I have? Who else do I have?

I thought through my words before I spoke. "Mama Tudora," I sputtered out. My throat was sore as though kittens rose from my stomach to scratch inside and leave their mark.

She stopped and lifted a bowl to my lips. "Drink this first, boy, before you speak," she said with excitement.

I drank down the soothing tea—some bitter-sweet taste mixed with sour. She set the bowl down on the chair behind her. She brushed back my hair.

"Oh, it will be fine to have you speak. Tata Grigore will be back from summer camp soon. The weather begins to cool. He will be so happy to see how well you are doing. I want your name first." She bent down to my face.

"Voicu," I said with a muffled stutter. "I am Voicu." I stopped to wet my lips. "I ran from Dracula's castle. The Turks were coming and I did not want to be a slave. I helped in the kitchen."

"The Turks would have killed you—if not Dracula! I know some would say otherwise, but I always have thought him to be of the Devil. Oh, Voicu, do you have a family?"

"No. I have no one."

Just then, we heard bells. Mama Tudora ran outside. I heard her yelling "Grigore! Grigore! Oh, Grigore, you're back!"

"Ho-oh! Ho-oh! Ho-oh!" He sang back. Sheep bleated and scrambled as they were herded into a corral outside. A dog barked and Grigore shouted, but the sound I heard most between him and his wife was laughter.

The dog ran in first. His wet nose sniffed my face and then he licked and licked and licked.

"Does the boy live?" asked Grigore as he stepped inside with a grin.

"Oh, just wait! He is doing so well. You will see. And just now he spoke! He is called Voicu." Mama Tudora held Grigore's hand and led him to my bed.

"Voicu, I am Grigore." He grasped my hand.

"Hello." My voice was rough. I squinted upwards. The light caused my eyes to tear, but there was something else. Something about his eyes?

"Oh, Voicu you should not be talking yet. Did she bring it out in you?" He looked at his wife. "Are you forcing him to speak to keep you entertained?"

"Now, Grigore, he has no family. I told him he must call you Tata Grigore and me Mama Tudora."

"No family?" He raised an eyebrow at me. I nodded. He was a strong-looking man—stocky in build and long with a beard. He, too, was graying with hair more of dirt color. Why does he look familiar?

CHAPTER 5

Healing

Good and evil—do I truly know one from the other? I have lived with my lies for so very long. Petra's ears twitch in the cool damp air.

The decision is one I must make alone. Which path should I take? Only two exist. Either I tell the truth or I live a life based on deceit. I should not fear the truth, but I know what it may bring—death. Yes, he was right, death is everywhere but so is love. This is why I sit here. On this silent night, I am asking God which path—which path should I take?

***

The house filled with the laughter of Tudora and Grigore. I have never met two more in love. At times, I think they forgot me completely. It was like this the whole night. I fell in and out of sleep. Darkness held the sounds of sheep moving with bells jingling. Above in the loft, I heard soft talking, laughter, and groans. I knew what the groans were from. Once I heard it coming from the servant's quarters behind the kitchen. I had asked Matei about it and he laughed, "They are making babies." I wandered off into the courtyard and asked some of the guards about "making babies" and they laughed too. Then they slapped me on the back and said, "One day you will impale a woman too!" and "It is for your father to tell you about."

Well, I did not ask Father about it, but I asked Mama. She said, "It happens when you marry. It is necessary and good. You will understand better when you are older." I trusted Mama, but my curiosity about it all grew. I could not stop thinking about it. So I went back to Matei and Voicu one night. They explained about a man and a woman naked and how things fit together. It was strange to me, but later in the week one of the stallions got loose from the stable and found his way to a mare. I saw him mount her and then I understood. Anyhow, this was the noise from above. I wondered if they wanted children. Were they too old? Then I wondered further, in part because of the clothing Mama Tudora gave me—do they have other relatives somewhere? Then, I fell sound asleep.

"What can we do, but help the boy," Mama Todora spoke in the dark of early morn. Her husband shuffled in his chair. I peeked out from under my sheepskin. They sat at the table, even before the sun had risen. "He is a gift from God," she said patting his hand.

"How can we feed him? As he grows, he will eat more and more." Tata Gigore was sensible.

"Yes, but once he heals he will be useful. I can tell. He is a good child. And if he worked in the castle kitchen, then he must have some skills. Oh, and think, by spring he will be able to help you with the flock. I would be so much happier if you were not out on the mountain so alone. Oh, Grigore, you will see."

I heard padded feet stepping in my direction. It was Petra. His wet muzzle touched my face. He licked and licked until I groaned.

"Good morning, Voicu." Grigore laughed.

"We do not have a rooster to wake you, so Petra will have to do," Mama Tudora giggled.

"Good morn," I responded reaching out to pet Petra. "Mama Tudora."

"Oh, is it time?" She grabbed my bowl. "Here." She handed it to Grigore. "He cannot walk out. Be useful, while I fix a little breakfast for Voicu and his legs."

Grigore raised an eyebrow, "I have milked a sheep, but never a boy."

"Get over there or I will have you clean his bed," She patted his backside.

When Mama Tudora finished boiling some mix, I drank it down. "Today, we will change your leggings and I will rub your legs down. They will heal up soon. You will see."

Then I realized how effective her nursing was. My pain was much less. And, I noted, I could wiggle my toes. She and Grigore together removed my mud casts. After all, broke away, Grigore inspected it with hesitation. He breathed deeply. "Oh, will they ever heal?"

"You! Do not think so! They will heal. At this point, we will have to change his cast more often—little by little. You did not see when I first began. Already it is so much better. And there is no infection." She rubbed ointment up and down my legs. They were left open to the air.

She beckoned Grigore closer. "Your job is to keep all the flies away while this dries. I will not have anything lay eggs in those wounds."

"Yes." Grigore nodded. He sat next to my bed. With his old felt hat in hand, he swooshed as he spoke, "Do you want to hear a story?"

"Yes," I was eager for a distraction and bored.

"This is a story told to me by my Tata. His Tata may have told to him. I do not know when it happened—so do not ask. It is a story from the past. Will you stay awake enough to hear it? It is not too long."

"Yes, Tata," I surprised myself with my words.

He smiled patting me on my arm.

"Long, long ago here on this mountain was a boy. His name was Mircea. He was of your age. It may even be he was Roman. It was so long ago. The people of the village took care of him. Like you, he had no family. So, they fed him and gave him clothing, and took him into their homes. In return, he would watch their flocks and he was a very good Shepherd.

"There was another boy named Novac. He envied Mircea. He did not like the other boy coming to town and having everyone welcome him. Whenever Mircea returned from the mountain with the flocks, he was fed well and loved by everyone. Novac wished the townspeople would love him instead. You must know you cannot force such matters.

"Novac was lazy and evil. Why should they love him? Even the animals around town ran when he came down the street. And, although this was not the kind of attention Novac wanted—it felt powerful to have the animals run away. It felt even more powerful when the little children ran and hid from him.

"So, when the good Shepherd, Mircea, came to town, Novac would seek him out.

"'You are weak and smell of sheep,' said Novac and this was an insult.

"Mircea smiled and said, 'Here. Take some of my bread, so we can be friends.'

"'You are weak. Why would I be your friend?' asked Novac. He pushed the Shepherd boy over into the dirt. Laughed at his strength and thought himself powerful.

"Mircea brushed off himself and his bread saying, 'I will not hold this against you. Let us be friends.'

"And this is how it went for a very long time. The bad boy would seek out the Shepherd and mock him. He would fight him and beat him but still, Mircea said, 'Let us be friends.'

"The events did not go without notice from the town people. As Novac grew, so, too, his anger grew. The people of the town ran and hid whenever he came down the street. The King heard stories and sought out Novac who was now a man.

"'Will you be my advisor and spokesman to the people?' asked the selfish King. 'I have heard the town people fear you and so with your power, you will increase my wealth and yours.'

"Soon, Novac came into town with a fancy uniform given to him by the King. He also had some soldiers who came to help collect his and the king's wealth from the people. For those who did not heed his words, he made a sport of torture and killing.

"With his wealth, he had a huge villa built. He had a beautiful wife and several fat children. When he went to his wife, she would say 'Yes, I will make this happen, if you buy me a new ring.' His children were the same. They would cry, 'If you love me, you will buy me this pony.' And Novac thought this was how to show his love. He gave them everything and these children began to become as evil and lazy as their Tata.

"You are wondering what happened to the Shepherd, Mircea. He continued to be cared for by the whole town. Love for him grew. He also had a wife. She was a plain but good woman. Together they built a simple shack in the hills. They had several children also. He, his wife, and his children were very, very happy.

"Mircea did not hesitate to give freely to the king. Novac increased the amount he took each time. As the town folk grew in poverty, he grew in wealth. He felt powerful. But when he came to collect with his gruff face and aging fat body, he would see the happiness of Mircea's simple family. He couldn't help but feel bitter. As he and his soldiers went to leave, the Shepherd would smile with, 'Let us be friends'. Novac would wave his hand and look away.

"Then, after some time, Novac fell out of favor with the King. In the change of one season, he lost his money, his house, and even his family. His health became worse. His beautiful clothing turned to rags. He begged in the street and few took pity on the once cruel man. Women would spit at him and dogs would piss on him. He was truly pathetic.

"Mircea found Novac one day lying in the gutter with no strength. He looked down at the poor soul and reached out saying, 'let us be friends.'

"The once bad boy, then Advisor to the king, then beggar reached up with his little strength. He agreed, 'Yes, let us be friends.' And with this simple act of love, life changed for both. The two became the best of friends and, for the once bad, life was never so good. It was a simple but powerful choice." Then, Grigore brushed my hair from my eyes, "Always be good in life, Voicu, and life will be good for you."

"Thank you, Tata Grigore." I thought about this story and what Tata had said and then I slept a very deep sleep. When I woke, my leg casts were new, and felt much better. Little by little my health improved.

The days went on and soon winter came with snow and ice. The cold wind would blow into the home whenever Grigore or Tudora opened the door. It seemed they were always running here and there—gathering wood or carrying water. My healing continued and progress appeared to leap. By the Christmas celebration, I was sitting up.

On Christmas Eve, we sang carols. We had a warm drink and were merry. Grigore looked at me. "I have something to give to you, Voicu. It is a gift. Not much, but soon they will be handy." He ran outside and came in with some crutches cut and carved from saplings. "Here. I hope I have measured them well."

"Oh, Tata, they are a wonder!" I sat and held one in each hand. The smooth wood was cold from sitting outside and felt like icicles.

"Your Mama Tudora has a gift as well." I noticed a quiet look between Tata and Mama as she climbed the stairs up into the loft. She soon came down with a stack of clothing. "These are for you—some trousers, a shirt, and a skin coat. I also have some boots and felt slippers. I will make certain you will not be cold."

I sputtered, "All this for me. But I have nothing for you."

Tata leaned toward me. "We are happy for your company."

"And to see these clothes in use again." Mama poked at the fire in the hearth.

"Again?" I asked.

"Oh, Grigore, it is not right to keep it from him."

"Da, you may tell." Tata sat down behind her.

Mama looked with teary eyes into mine. "Voicu, these clothes were our son's. He grew into a man."

"You have a son. Does he live near?" From the sadness on their faces, I regretted my words.

"No! No! No! Not on Christmas!" Grigore stomped out the door. Tudora followed.

The cold wind coming from outside blew my hair across my eyes. Through the window slit, I could see them standing in the distance. Their hands moved as they spoke loud words to each other. A blue moonlight reflected off the snow. I heard words shouted in the wind and then, as loud, sobbing. Grigore pulled Tudora close. Their bodies shook together as they cried upon each other. I have never felt such sadness. It was like this for some time. Oh, it made my body, mind, and heart ache! Something so terrible had happened—too sad to share with anyone other than your truest love.

I wanted to brighten them. I wanted to show I cared. It was this want that made me do it. I'm certain Mama Tudora wouldn't have allowed me to so soon. I took the crutches and put them under my arms. Then, I slide my bottom to the edge of the bed. I was without shoes, but the dirt felt good again on the bottom of my feet. I slide down putting my weight on them. It hurt some, but not as much as I thought it would. I inched along the bed to the wall. I carefully kept my weight on my buttocks and crutches. I inched sliding with my backside against the wall.

The door had a simple pull and, with some effort, I opened it. The cold night air filled my lungs, as I eased out onto the rampway. I noticed the icy path and thought it better not to make my fall certain. I stopped. The fireplace and candles glowed behind my weak body and the wind nearly blew me over. I looked out and shouted as loud as my lungs would allow. "Mama Tudora! Tata Grigore! Come visit!"

Chapter 6

Spring Strength

I lift my pant cuffs and scratch at my wood hard legs. The scars web off from lumps where the bones healed. I remember the first spring well. Petra licks my thigh and I laugh, "No boy that tickles!" I have still to decide. Yes or no. Up or down. Truth or lies. I remember.

My first walk gave Mama Tudora a scare. Grigore was behind and held her skirt as he slid. "Slow down, my horse, slow down!" He laughed as she slapped him with one hand.

"He will fall, Grigore, he will fall!" she held her hand over her mouth.

"He will not fall! Woman, slow down to a canter," Tata Gigore laughed.

Then they both held hands and carefully stepped along the icy stones of the walkway up to me.

I stayed steady but when Grigore asked if he could help I said, "Please." He lifted me straight up and heaved me over to my bed.

I used the crutches every day from then on. At first, Mama Tudora was very strict. "I do not want to have to heal your legs again. Take care." With time, her words changed. "I think you can walk further." Then she began to make orders. "Get some wood" or "fetch the water" were constant commands. I followed her directions as quickly as I could. She always kissed me on the cheek after I completed a chore.

My arms and legs grew strong. The daylight stayed longer and snow and ice began to disappear.

I traveled to the corral, to the streambed, and to an old oak tree beyond the corral, with my crutches. The smell of sheep was strong outside. The ram met me at the rails of their containment and lifted his lips in a smile as he guarded his ewes. "He likes me, Tata." I filled the manger with hay.

"Yes, he likes you—but he likes everyone. Spring is in the air," declared Tata. He was silent and lost in thought then suggested, "Let us go for a walk while Mama is dying her wool. We can talk." I noted the snow and ice giving way to wet patches and slush as I followed. Tata Grigore did not slow as I scurried to stay in his shadow. He expected me to keep at his pace. Following the stream, we scared some wild beasts further into the underbrush. The sun poked through the forest and sent sliced shadows across the snow.

"Come now." He beckoned. "We will rest ahead."

We climbed up. Then, up further. I know Mama Tudora would not have approved.

"A little more," he prompted.

I stumbled with my crutches. Once or twice I slid some but did not tell Tata.

"Almost there." His smile pulled me along.

My lungs felt sore with strained breath and my arms shook from the weight of my body against the crutches.

"Ah, yes! The sun has warmed our seat." Grigore stepped up onto a huge flat rock surface that jutted out with a cliff edge looking down to a half-ice-covered river far below.

We sat on the rock. I set my crutches aside and sucked air into my lungs.

Dracula's Son

"Here is my spot. I come here to think—sometimes about the sheep—sometimes about Mama. The answer I need always comes. This is a special spot. God sends me the light and gives me a seat and, with time, the answer I seek. I have simply to listen."

I nodded. "Do you have a question today?"

"Yes, but it is not for God." He turned towards me. "It is for you."

"Ask me and I will answer," I responded.

"Good. I have only one request—honesty." Then he looked straight at me. His eyes probed, like a hawk looking for a mouse, into my soul. I swear he could see whether I was telling the truth. "After I found you, I returned to the spot where you fell. The sheep were grazing and I explored the cranny of rocks climbing higher and higher—a difficult climb but I found a way. It may have been a week since your fall—maybe, even longer. Still, I found horse tracks. I counted five but saw more. So, I wondered. You did not mention stealing a horse. You said you escaped alone. And, these tracks went down the slope—in the direction of Dracula's castle. It has confused me since you fell into our world. Please, Voicu, explain these things I saw."

I hesitated in thought. How can I tell the truth? If Tata and Mama knew who I was what would they think? Would I be in danger? Would I put them in danger? I remembered my true father's words. 'Tell no one who you are until you are in Hungary' he said. So, I lied in some way, "Could these have appeared later by someone in search of me?"

He let out a sigh, "They could have." Tata Grigore nodded ever so slightly. He sat in silence as though waiting for me to speak further. The pain in my legs was small compared to the pain I felt from keeping the truth.

"It was dark when I fell from the cliff. I was tired and confused. I should have been more careful. There is little more I can say except I am happy to be alive," I looked away down the river flow below. I knew when I fully healed, I would need to leave and travel to Hungary. It would not be easy and I do not know if my father would welcome my presence. I would travel alone.

He said nothing but his silence told me all—he knew I was not speaking the truth. I could see a tear forming in the corner of his eye. Maybe it is the sunlight, I told myself, but I knew. Tata was disappointed. He knew I lied.

Chapter 7

The Cleansing

Soon, I shuffled around without the crutches. With health came more responsibilities. I helped Mama Tudora with her many chores. We collected firewood, gathered fresh herbs, and cleaned the house. I also helped Tata Grigore with the sheep.

With springtime came many new lambs. I spent my time watching Tata as he worked with the sheep. I helped him with feeding and leaned against the corral. Petra was always near. He kept a constant eye on the woods watching for other animals—especially the hungry wolves.

"One day you will be a great Shepherd." Tata looked over as I cleaned a newborn lamb and put its head below the mother's teats to suckle.

"There is so much to know. I could never be the Shepherd you are."

"We will see. You have been working hard, Voicu. I want you to relax for the rest of the day. You can go for a swim and bathe in the stream. I will move the flock out of the meadow and back into their corrals for the evening. Later, I will join you. Mama Tudora will be happier having both of us well-cleaned!"

I did as Tata said. I went down to the stream. The water came splashing over the boulders above and into the pool below. A breeze meandered through the trees and everything smelled new.

I stripped my clothes off and hung them folded over a bush. First, I had one foot in and then the other. I slide along the smooth rocks on the bottom. I tried to step without slowing but, as the waters deepened, it was harder to move into the current. I stood on my tiptoes when the water rose to my crotch; this caused me to lose my balance and I fell back into the water. Oh, it was cold and it took my breath for a moment.

I stood up again coughing water out of my mouth and nose. I plugged one nostril and blew snot out. I did the same with the other. I dove into the deeper pool and my body adjusted to the cool waters. I swam around while minnows nibbled at my cloudy white feet.

Then, for some reason, my mind fell back in time. My heart raced and my throat tightened. My breathing became strained like I imagine one being buried alive might fight for air. I floated out of my body remembering the last time I swam in the river below the castle. The current was stronger and swifter. I heard screaming and splashing far upstream somewhere near the castle. I was out in the deepest part of the pool far from shore in slow waters.

As I paddle swam, the river changed to the color of blood. I panicked! Everything changed like a storm arriving without warning. I couldn't get out, as the body came bouncing over the rocks in the flow—the dead and dying everywhere! They surrounded me. Some were against me. One grabbed me. I screamed for help. It was a woman. Her breast area sliced from her body and she appeared more like a monster. It made me sick. Taking in water tasting of blood, I kept swimming and bodies everywhere bounced by. They were warm and some cut in two. I gave way to thoughts of floating high above looking down. Frogs—all they are is frogs, I told myself.

The sound of the current drowned out any sound from them as they floated on. I got to shore and watched them heading down the river. The strangest thing though is as I looked at them they changed into frogs. I swear they did. Yes, they are just frogs!

"Swim, frogs, swim!" This is what I yelled laughing from my rock platform at the river's edge. Sir Stefan found me hugging my legs and repeating, "Swim, frogs, swim! Swim, frogs, swim!"

"Young Master, look at me! You do not know what you are saying. Look at me!" pleaded Sir Stefan. He picked me up and I laughed. "Good Mihnea, let us go away and let them float down to the river of death."

Then I reentered my body back in the mountain pool. I laughed madly. Then I spotted them—the frogs. They sat on the other shore and one jumped in. Oh, how I hate frogs!

I searched to find the proper branches. I hunted as a silent predator waiting for them to swim close. First one caught—then two. Soon I had eight fine frogs. I impaled them just as my father might have. I lined them at the stream's edge in a soft mud area. They slide up and down on their sticks trying to get away. Their eyes bulged. Bubbles popped from their mouths. I laughed and laughed. Then I heard the fast rhythm of padded feet. Petra came at full speed into the mud and sniffed the frogs. I jumped back into the deep water. I remembered those times with my Father—Fear. Oh the power in fear!

"Boy, what have you done?" Tata Grigore yelled so fiercely it caused me to tense. He looked at me first with sadness and then paused and looked away.

His voice calmed. "Get up here, Son. Get dressed and then (he pointed to the frog) get your dinner. Mama and I are cooking mutton stew. There will not be enough for you. None of us kills God's creatures without a reason, so it is a good thing you caught your dinner. We do not know how to cook a frog, but you being kitchen help should have no problem making your fine food. Mama and I do not eat such things, but we will watch to see your expert cooking. Then we will watch you eat them."

I swallowed hard as I saw Grigore tromp away with anger toward the house. Is he serious? I slipped into my pants and pulled my shirt overhead. I tied my sandals and then stepped over rocks upstream and eased over to the frogs. One by one, I pulled up the frogs on their sticks. Several were still moving. What had I done? Am I turning into a madman?

Maybe I could leave for Hungary tonight. Maybe, I could escape. My legs were not well enough though. I may not make it and I did not know what fate waiting for me upon my arrival. I held my knees close and rocked. Was I crazy? I sat for some time by the stream deep in thought.

I hiked back carrying the frogs and realized I would have to pretend to know how to cook. How bad could they be? I could ask Mama Tudora for some herbs. I could clean them with some water and cut off their heads. I would have to be convincing and confident. I could make them believe. I was certain I could act like the cooks I had seen in the kitchen so often. Yes, I would cook these frogs and they would taste good!

***

Reflecting on this night, I laugh at myself. Mama Tudora would later tell me she could hardly keep from bursting. That night she and Tata laughed themselves to sleep in the comfort of their loft. My night had not been so restful.

***

Tata Grigore stood at the front of the house. The sheep circled in the corral, as I laid the frogs on sticks out in the grass.

"I have started a small fire for your roasting. Mama and I will be out to watch you do your cooking. Mama says she may someday cook some frogs too. Our simple food of mutton and turnips with dried apples has filled us. So, we will watch and learn," he stated.

I clapped my hands together and acted like I was a fine chef. "I will need some herbs and some bark from the wood pile."

"I will get you some bark." Tata bounced away grinning. "Mama, Voicu wants to have some herbs. Can you bring him the special ones?"

Later I would find out what the special herbs were. They were a very effective mix Mama Tudora had created for the times when Tata needed to relax his bowels.

Mama Tudora came running out. "Here are your herbs."

Thinking it would improve the taste of the frogs, I said, "Oh, I will need much more." I crumpled a pinch of the herbs under my nose.

"Much more?" asked Mama as she turned to Tata.

"Voicu is a cook, Tudora. Get him some more of the herbs!" Tata waved her back into the house.

She ran off and I yelled in, "I will need eight times as much. This is what will bring out their flavor. It is a special way to prepare taught to me by a famous cook from France. I must have plenty of herbs."

Mama Tudora looked out the doorway, "Eight times the amount?"

"Yes, or more," I clarified.

I took the frogs from their sticks and cleaned out their insides.

"Oh," said Grigore looking over my shoulder, "I thought the French kept the insides for flavor."

"Only some do. This cook did not. 'The inside space is to be filled with the herbs,' he said…only in French."

"You speak French too?" said Tata. "Alors mange tes grenouilles maintenant!"

"No. He spoke through an interpreter, Now, I wrap the frogs in the bark. You see between two pieces." I rubbed my hands together and licked my lips. "These will be delicious!"

"Oh, yes." Mama stepped closer. "How long do you cook them?"

I explained, "They must be cooked fully. I let the bark burn completely." I figured by burning them and eating mostly the herbs, the taste would be bearable.

Mama and Tata watched me with fascination. I turned the bark-covered frogs with two large sticks.

"Let me get you a bowel. I mean bowl." Mama giggled as she ran inside.

Then, one by one, I loaded the frogs into the bowl. They would not taste so bad.

"You will eat all eight?" Tata said more like a command and less like a question.

"Of course, I will eat all of them. They are so small only eight can fill someone growing like me. But I can share," I offered one to Mama with my more sincere smile.

"Oh, Tata and I are so full. We would not think of taking any of your French delicacies. But, mind us not, as we watch you eat," Mama Tudora folded her hands inspecting every single move and I felt as though I was an actor in a play.

I sat and stopped to say my prayers. Then, I picked up my first frog. The legs were chewy and charred; they took much effort to swallow. Mama and Tata sat big-eyed and silent whenever I peeked in their direction.

"How does your cooking taste?" Tata smiled from his seat.

"Ummm! It is delicious! Could I bother you Mama for a mug with water?"

"Oh, certainly," she hurried to fill a mug from a nearby bucket.

But Tata did not go. No, he did not. He sat strong-eyed with folded arms and watched me. I continued my performance willing myself to eat without stopping. I smiled as I ate the very last of all the frogs. They were terrible in taste and texture, but I could not let them know. I would pretend it was the best meal ever. I belched causing my eyes to water. "This is what the French do when they finish with a good meal. They burp."

"I see." Tata had a wise, understanding look in his eye. "Now, Voicu, the next time you wish to go hunting, you will let one of us know. This is a rule. God would not want any of his creation killed without a reason."

"Yes, Tata. And, next time, I will hunt enough for all of us."

Mama stood in the doorway and seemed to laugh or was she just coughing?

"Tomorrow, we will go to high pasture. It is the right time of the year. We must fatten the sheep so they are ready for Summer Market. We will be up before the sun."

"Yes, Tata." I did not know I would not sleep at all the full night. Maybe the frogs had their revenge?

I lay down in the soft moss near the corral. Petra was near. I reached over to scratch his ears, "Oh, Petra, I do not feel so well." He perked his ears, arose, and wandered into the night. I rolled over shaking and felt droplets of sweat fall from my brow. My breath was strained. Movement, breath, everything was exhausting and I felt weak. I searched for the stars but they appeared unfamiliar and started to move and swirl in among the trees. Why are the stars doing that? My stomach oh! Then there was a rumble deep inside and I pushed myself up from the ground. A voice unlike any I had ever heard came from every direction or, maybe, from no direction—choose love or fear. It came again as I rushed into the forest and held myself up by leaning again an old pine—love or fear? A rush of frog bits and acid littered the soft ground. Love or fear? Did I want to be like my true father or did I want to become a man dedicated to love and not fear? The lights danced overhead. Love or fear? Then I spotted Mama among the lights. Love or fear? There was Voicu. Love or fear? Love or fear? Then the rumble moved from my stomach and dropped lower. Love or fear? "Ahhhhh!"

I rushed to a fallen log, dropped my pants, and shat endlessly into a bed of leaves. Oh, my arse! Then I vomited again. Love or fear? The lights continued to sway among the canopy of the forest shooting in every direction as though playing some childhood game. The night continued this way. I could not decide which part of me burnt the most. Just as I considered I must have cleared out everything I carried inside, more would find a way out. Love or fear?—I considered as I wiped the sweat from my forehead and watched the lights continue to dance. Love or fear. There is only one choice—love. I choose love.

As though the fog cleared, my symptoms exited throughout the night. I did vomit and shat a little more, but eventually, it subsided. I choose love. I did not entirely recognize myself. I was a new man. Yes, I had been a boy, but in choosing my life direction I felt I had become a man. I once was a spoiled boy shouting my way through the halls of a castle, but now was a man dedicated to hard work, loyalty, honesty, and sincerity. I moved from visions of death and dying to only seeing and knowing visions of love and life. I went from frogs to no frogs. The frogs were gone except for an occasional sighting along the stream. All of these vomiting runs, chills and sweatings cleaned me. I was like a dry bone found along a path. I was nothing. Except there was one spark. Love. This would become the new fire I would kindle—love.

I did dream for a short while. It was my Mama. She radiated. She shone! In all her beauty still wearing her red gown, she took my hand, "You are not to blame. Open your heart to love. The frogs can go free! Let them free! No more will you carry the burden. Your father's sins are not your own." I could feel it as though some large boulder floated off my chest. I was free to love. I was free to release my past.

In the morning, I was so tired but had this deep, deep knowledge—I had cleared the frogs from me forever. I would never kill another. I would never dream of them again. The frogs were gone!

Chapter 8

High Meadow

I had my full strength and more, as spring became summer. My breaks had healed like Roman concrete. Some mornings I would wake expecting to be in my soft bed of childhood. To some, it would sound a contradiction, but once I realigned my mind to my new life, often helpfully reminded by a morning kiss from Petra, I would up myself from bed feeling alive and happier than I can ever remember. I did not miss being a child of royalty. Yes, I did miss my true Mama but the fears and nightmares of childhood need never return. I was happier and felt more freedom in the mountains and poor life of a shepherd than ever as the spoiled child of a dark-hearted prince. I learned to tend the sheep. I could herd and corral them, with the help of Petra. Mama Tudora showed me medicinal plants. These could help the sick sheep when they were weak, skinny, or seemed lost from the flock. I hadn't realized, how much I would need to learn, but I learned little by little.

One morning as Tata, Petra, and I stood together watching the flock Tata Grigore spoke of the grazing, "We stand in the near meadow. The high meadow and mountain meadow are above us. We take them to where the grasses are tall." He motioned his arm and pointed far off to a high field beyond the woods and waters but a clear climb from where we stood.

"When will we go to the mountain meadow?" I asked.

"I let the grasses grow there. We will go mid-summer. Then the sheep will be good and fat for the late Summer Market in Arafu," he scanned the far-away greens high above.

"We will go to town?" I asked.

"Yes, we will need to go to market. This year our flock is so large, that we will take over one hundred beasts! We will have enough money to afford our town supplies for the year. And, we will all get some new clothes. I want to surprise Mama with some new bowls." Tata skipped over to a wandering yearling with great cheer.

The high meadow was not so far from home. The grasses were tall when we first arrived. The sheep loved grazing and grew round. After a full month of grazing and moving the flock about all left of the meadows was but green stubble.

When mid-summer came, we traveled high into the mountains. Way up where Tata had first found me. At night, we slept under the stars. Always, we listened for Petra's bark which signaled wolves were near.

The wolves kept some distance, usually. They came close though one night. Tata and I were warming by the flames. I saw only one at first. I could see the reflection from its eyes, as it was close enough to the glow of the fire. At once Petra, Tata, and I jumped into action.

"Watch them, Voicu. Watch them!" Tata ordered.

"Will they jump at us?"

"I have seen this happen. We will have to split up. You and Petra go to the low side of the flock. I will stay here. Take my staff."

"Tata, I will my use own. It is more my size and you will need yours." I picked up the smooth staff I had carved from a knobby birch sapling.

We ran down to the dark side of the flock. Tata threw all the wood onto the fire. It snapped and glowed high up into the trees and forest surrounding the meadow. I looked about and counted fourteen of the howling beast.

"Petra stay close. We may be fighting them off." I beckoned him closer with the motion of my hand.

We circled. A wolf came close and sniffed the ground, within a body length of one of our fat ewes. We charged him. Petra was in front. I pretended my staff was a sword. I swirled, thrust, and made an upward slice. I hit the wolf's side and, with a yelp of pain, it scurried into the dark of the forest.

We carried on through the night. The wolves came towards us, building confidence with every approach. They outnumbered us, but we were wiser and charged with the task of protecting. I was so very tired and I could see Tata was feeling the same. How can we continue to keep the beast away? Then the pack turned their heads to the sound of something approaching. "Koo-koo-low! Koo-koo-low!" A strong voice came from the far forest. The wolves so feared the sound, that one side scattered to the safety of the dark. Then came another voice. "Oy-oy-ya! Oy-oy-ya!" This voice especially surprised me, as it was a girl. The two sounded like an army. Everywhere the wolves ran—some so disoriented they hurried towards us.

The man was huge and shaggy lumbering like a bear as he came from the dark. His eyes scanned from side to side and his staff swung like the great tower bell! An omen of doom. He hit one, then another, then another of the mad animals.

The girl continued her war cry of "Oy-oy-ya!" and then I spotted the quiver over one shoulder and the delicate lines of a bow over the other. Pulling an arrow quick as lightning, she drew the bow and released it straight into one of the larger wolves. She circled the flock from the bottom coming round closer towards me. I guessed she stood a full head shorter than I. She nodded and I returned the nod. Then we focused on fighting. The wolves did not come much more. They seemed to understand their efforts would prove fruitless.

But one seemed mad and charged from the darkness towards me. I lifted my staff ready to fight him off. He came full speed with massive muscles bulging. His jaws snapped snarling. I heard a whoosh! as he pounced at me in full force. My staff would not fend off such efforts and I waited for his claws and teeth to rip me open. The body fell on me; it was dead. I tumbled trying to push the massive twitching weight of the carcass off. The girl had shot an arrow straight through the monster's neck. Blood was about the fur and I squirmed underneath the stinking beast. She took large strides over and then she did something I will always remember. It impressed me. She reached down and pulled her arrow from the fur mound and licked it off. "A good kill and I do not like my arrows dirtied." Then she pranced off with swaying hips.

I lifted with all my strength and finally rolled the carcass off. "Hold on," I said. "What is your name?"

"Dumitra. Dumitra Florina—the Flower." she calmly looked off to the horizon. "The sun rises. The wolves will take shelter in the shadows." Then she wandered off without another word.

Tata was with the giant.

"You found this boy?" The man had a deep bearish voice.

"Da. He escaped from the castle before the Turks came," Tata explained.

"Ha! He was not the only one to escape the Sultan. Vlad Tepes also outwitted the Turks. He and some of his men made it to the King in Hungary and were tossed into prison—as deserved! We cannot have the Sultan take control but it is as though one demon fights another." He held out his enormous hand towards me. "Call me Barbu. You have already met my daughter, Dumitra."

"Yes. My name is Voicu." I thought for a moment of his words. My father was now imprisoned. I would face the same fate if I ventured to Hungary. I have nowhere to go.

"I saved him, Tata." Dumitra nodded in my direction.

"Why you were not born a boy, I do not understand." Barbu looked down at his daughter. "Sure, she can cook and clean, but she also can hunt and fish and even tend the sheep."

"Who is with your flock now?" asked Tata Grigore.

"My brother, Andrei, is back with them. When we saw your fire across the forest, we thought the wolves had begun giving you trouble, so we came." Barbu leaned against his staff.

"And we thank you." Tata slapped Barbu on the shoulder.

"Yes, thank you." I shook the giant's hand.

"With daylight, we must go back to our sheep," said Barbu. "We are on the other side of the forest if you need our help."

"Likewise, my friend—we, too, are at your service," Tata bowed.

The summer went on and in the deep green hillsides, the sheep grew fat. Petra and I spent our days resting on the uphill side of the flock and Tata downhill. We met midday to eat and make plans.

"We will move the flock again tomorrow. It is less than one week until Summer Market. Oh, we should have a fine year." Tata smiled contently.

"How many days will we need to get the flock down?" I asked.

"It takes about three. We will not take all of the sheep. The yearlings, my best two rams, and several dozen ewes will stay for our new flock. It will take time to build our numbers again—but we will."

At night the sky began to swirl with storm clouds. Sounds, as though Hell were crashing around the mountain, grew more intense. A flash of light filled the air with crackles and heavy rain. I could see Tata below as he fought to keep his stance. He leaned on his staff fighting the downpour and the winds.

Petra and I huddled together. I kept my eyes alert for any action from the herd. The sheep came close together from fear and were easier to watch this way. They did not concern themselves with eating. They huddled together bleating from time to time. Like us, they fought off the winds and constant downpours. A mountain chill took the storm winds and still it did not quite freeze. Tata stood alone, not moving from his spot.

In the early morning light, the air was a sea of drizzle. I rushed down to Tata and feared what I saw. He was pale—the color of a dead body.

"Tata, what is wrong?" He did not answer but coughed and looked at me with bloodshot eyes. Then he fell over. I reached down and saw he was shaking.

"Petra, watch the flock," I ordered. Then I remembered one of Tata's lessons. His body was losing heat. He could die if I did not share some of my own body's heat. I lie on top of him and cover us both with my sheepskin. The shivers did not subside. The rains continued and I thought they might never stop.

"I will not let you die! Tata, listen to me. You need to stay awake. You need to stay with me through this storm. When the sun comes, we will dry out."

Then I heard a far-off sound, "Oy! Oy! Oy!" It was Dumitra. She must have seen us. Soon I heard the sound of splashing steps.

"Voicu, you need to get him to shelter. Take him down. I am warm and dry. I will tend to your sheep. Take him down and get Mama Tudora to care for him. Hold him up as you journey down the mountain path. You must be strong. Petra will help me. Go now!" ordered Dumitra.

I did as she said. I held him in place around the waist and he leaned against my side. He carried most of his weight. By some miracle, the rain slowed to a fine mist as I sloshed and half-dragged Tata through the mud and puddles. I kept a solid rhythm, not slowing or quickening my pace. Tata drifted towards sleep at times and I shook him awake each time.

"Tata, just a little further. Just a little further." He stumbled. We fell into the bramble and soft mud many times. I prayed in silence. I kept my strength and willed not to drop Tata again. This was the same path in which he had carried me to save my life, I would do the same. I lost the thought of pain and time. I focused willing the beating of my feet never stop. I yelled as we neared the house, "Mama! Help, Mama!"

Mama Tudora came running out the door. "Oh, Grigore! Oh, no! Get him inside! Get him inside, now!" She ran off to the woods.

Huffing through the doorway with a bundle of fresh herbs, Mama returned. "Voicu, what happened?"

"The storm overwhelmed him," my voice was just above a whisper.

"Help me to give him some tea," said Mama.

I held up his pale blue head and he coughed out some phlegm. His looks were of someone so close, so very close to death.

"Grigore, you listen! You will get better! I cannot have you dying on me." Mama said to Tata. He could not swallow on his own. Mama coxed his throat with one hand while she poured the warm liquid down with the other.

"Get him up on the bed," she ordered me, "and get all his wet clothes off." I followed her words. "I haven't time to be modest." She stripped her clothes off and jumped into bed with Tata. She hugged him close.

"Get the stack of sheepskins down from the loft. Bring them here, and trade your wet clothes out for some dry ones," she barked at me.

Tata started shivering in Mama's arms. "Good! Good, Grigore let your body warm up."

I came down to see Tata's color was changing again. He spits up over and over on Mama. I came over with a cloth and wiped her off. "It is okay. It is a good sign," she said softly and nodded toward the fire. "Eat some broth before you go. The sheep are waiting. Voicu, God willing, Tata will be well."

"What will we do about the Summer Market?" I asked as I built the fire up with more wood.

"It will be some time before Tata will be well enough to take such a journey. Go to the sheep and bring them back to the corral tomorrow." She closed her eyes, held Tata close, and gave him kisses.

My walking staff in hand, I strode out.

When I warily returned to the flock, it was not yet dark. Petra ran to greet me followed closely by Dumitra.

"Voicu, is your Tata well and warm?" asked Dumitra.

I pictured Mama snuggling with Tata. "Yes, he is warm and Mama tells me he will be well soon."

From out of the shadows behind Dumitra stepped Barbu.

"You will need help taking such a fine flock to the market. Tomorrow, we will start the journey with your Tata's flock. Andrei and Dumitra will take our flock. I will help you with yours. I owe your Tata a favor, this will repay it," said Barbu with his deep voice.

"Mama expects me to bring the sheep to the corral. She will not know what happened."

Barbu looked down at Dumitra. "Take your bow and quiver of arrows. You will deliver the message to Voicu's Mama Tudora. Spend the night and help. In the morning, fill her bin with wood and then leave to meet Uncle Andrei and the flock at the narrow pass. They will be there by midday, so you cannot be slow. Voicu and I will follow behind with the other flock."

"Yes, Tata." And then she left with a bounce running through the dark forest toward home. I thought of her as a woman. She carried herself with such strength and fearlessness. Yet, she could not have been any older than me. I watched losing my senses until Barbu slapped my shoulder.

"Watch your flock. I will come in the morning." He strode off in another direction.

I sat up late with thoughts. Will Tata be well again? Did the chills take him? Then I stopped myself. No. I need not think such things. I must focus on the flock. Mama Tudora would make him well again. It was certain.

The night was quiet with stars and deep ideas. It was a time when I wondered if God was looking down and focused on me. I sat and wondered and thought of all kinds of things. I leaned against a mound of grasses I had made. Then I did what a Shepherd must never do alone; I fell asleep.

With the morning light, I realized my mistake. The sheep had wandered and with Petra's help, I was able to fix the situation. Thank God none were taken by the wolves. When Barbu arrived, I was without breath.

"What's wrong, Voicu?" asked Barbu.

"Nothing."

"Ha! You fell asleep didn't you?" He squeezed my shoulder with a smile.

"Yes. Please don't let Tata know."

"Speaking of your father, I have had a change of thought. We will take the flock down by your parents' home. I want you to be able to check on him before we take the flock to town. Your Tata will be able to tell you which sheep should stay in the corral and which should go to market."

And so we directed the flock down the mountain. I must admit a kind of grave fear as we neared the quiet house. Barbu stayed with the flock in the field.

"Voicu!" Mama Tudora stood in the doorway. "Voicu, Tata has been asking for you. Please come and see. I told you he would be well—and he will." Her tired smile and weary eyes showed honest exhaustion.

I gave her a big hug, and then I hurried into the doorway with my hat in my hand.

"Tata, are you well?"

"Voicu, come close. I am still ill, but my healer will have me well soon." He appeared tired and, for the first time, old. His face brightened as he gripped my hand as though he had never been ill. "Oh, Voicu. God has been good to us. We had never thought we would ever have a son again—and then you came. I do think of you as my son. What would we do without you, now? Oh, you are a good boy." He took my shoulder and squeezed it with his hand. "Tudora. Come here." Tata said something to Mama in a whisper and she hurried off and up into the loft. She came down in an instant with a small box and handed it to Tata.

"Voicu, I have something very special I want to give to you. It is a gift." Then he started a kind of story, but it wasn't a story made up. It took me some time to realize, it was his story. He held the box in his hand. "One day long, long ago, a man and his son wandered through the woods on their way to market. Along the way, the man stumbled and slid down a short hill to a little cave opening. He looked inside and saw shining bright circles. He reached deep into the hole and came out with a surprise. By this time his son had come down to him and asked, 'What is it, Tata?' He showed him two coins. While the top of these ancient coins had no marks, on the back each had a perfect picture of a ram. You know, this was me and my son. We wrapped the coins and took them. A friend who works with metal fixed them with chains—one for each of us. We each wore them to remind ourselves we are only sheep and in need of protection. I put mine away when I was certain my boy had died."

My stomach felt as though it had risen into my throat. My heartbeat galloped. In my reddened ears, I hear a swish! Swish! Swish! He opened the box and like a tumbling river current, many memories came rushing back. My mind went blank for a moment. It was the same medallion offered to me, so very long ago. My hand reached for the coin and as I touched the cold metal I sensed some power emitting from this simple charm. Can Tata see my hand tremble?

"Voicu, I want you to wear this. You are my son. This is how I see it. This way, you will always have the protection of my love and God's will."

I took the rope and hung the medallion around my neck. And I said so very softly, "Thank you, Tata." I kissed his cheeks. There were tears as thick as blood streaming down my cheeks. Tata had tears too but with a smile.

Barbu and I began the long journey after sorting the sheep to be saved in the corral. I felt the weight of the medallion against my chest as I looked out at the flock in front of us. I had more love for Grigore and Tudora than I ever thought possible. Yes, I chose love.

Chapter 9

Summer Market

The trip to the market took three full days. Barbu led the way and I followed behind the flock.

I remembered being through Arefu twice before as a child and both times in a carriage. I peeked out at the streets, people and buildings. Mother did not let me out among the people, as I think she feared for my life.

As we approached, I could see the walls had mountainous towers marked each by a guild. One the blacksmiths, the leatherworkers, and even the beekeepers. Each supported the town's security. The walls were thick and high. The smell of sheep was strong, but other smells of horse and cattle and even some foods also filled the air.

"Go ask where we must bed our flock," Barbu called down to me from a tall boulder overlooking the sheep.

I strolled casually trying to act as though I fit in. It had been some time since I had been in such a crowd. I nodded to the guards with my cloak hood hung over my head, though I doubted anyone would recognize me. I was waved in. I wandered by women selling knitted socks at their doorsteps. Singers and jugglers entertained. A man danced with a bear. My senses were overwhelmed and I found it important to remain focused.

First, I thought, I must attend to Barbu's question. The town clock rang out the hour as I scrambled through the crowd looking for what or whom I did not know. I needed to speak to someone official—a Magistrate or such. We needed the answer for it was soon to be dark.

I approached a gate guard with, "Excuse me, sir. Who do I speak with to find a place to settle my flock?"

"You'll want to talk with Master Chatar. He's over there." He pointed to a man standing on a high platform with a girth equal nearly to his height.

I thanked the guard and wove my way toward Chatar. He stood between a platform for the sales and a boy who, by his size, I guessed must be his son. The sky had a crimson glow as I wandered across the town square.

"Sir, Master Chatar," I stepped close to the platform edge, "Can you tell me where to keep my flock?" I waited for his response.

"Boy, I am too busy to talk to the likes of you." He pointed some workers off to one corner of the square. "Keep it short." He looked down his warty nose.

"I have my father's flock outside of the gates. I come to ask. Where should we bed them?"

"Oh, you and your father think you will sell here. Do you? What's your name boy?"

I looked at his sneer dripping with a hatred I did not understand. His son mimicked the same repulsed look, standing behind and to the side of his father. The boy was large, but I guessed he must be only a year or two older than me.

"My name is Voicu. My father is sick." I stood tall. Then from some part of my past, I brought out my old haughtiness. "If you cannot answer my question, then you must not be the man I am looking for." I stared straight into his eyes without humility. Instantly, I realized my mistake—no Shepherd boy would talk this way to an elder and an important man. I should have thought better and played myself meek.

The man's face matched the sky in color and swelled. He looked like an apple about to fall from the tree. "Go get your father! I will not speak to a boy. I will give him an answer which he may not like and tell him to swat the pride out of you. Now, go, boy!"

I stood in silence thinking for an instant. Chatar's son, later I would find out his name was Lancu, picked up a rock and threw it at me full force. It struck above my eye and I fell to the ground. I hobbled back to the gate, feeling dazed but thinking it better not to get into a fight. Blood dripped down the side of my face and below my ear. I could feel with my hand the swelling of the bruise.

I heard the boy laughing in the distance as I limped away. I inhaled a slow deep breath. Something funny came to mind. I laughed. It was Tata's story of the two boys. I made a decision. I don't know why. It was a challenge for me—one day I will be this boy's friend.

By the time I had stumbled back to Barbu, I must have looked a sight. Dumitra stood next to him but came running when she saw what had happened. She grabbed a small wooden bowl and a rag from a satchel she was carrying. She dipped the rag in a bubbling spring under a nearby tree and handed it to me, "Hold this over it. I will get some herbs to help with the wound." She hurried off.

"Who did this to you?" Barbu made a shadow over me, as he looked down with fists against his waist.

"Master Chatar. I mean—the round boy standing next to him. Maybe his son?" I shrugged my shoulders.

"You think right. Oh, Lancu is a little demon. I will give them both a piece of my mind! They know better than to anger Barbu! Watch the sheep. I will be back shortly." He ambled off as though a mountain had sprouted legs and was appointed to fall upon the town to squash it. With his staff in hand, the crowd parted as they spotted him approaching. Barbu and his temper were legendary. I do not know what Barbu said. Nor do I know what he did within the gates. But soon, very soon, several boys with staff came out and found me. "We have instructions to help you get your flock into one of the town paddocks. They will be among the first to sell. What luck!" one of the smaller boys said.

So, as a group, we circled the flock, and with many "Hoo- Yas!" soon they were inside a fenced area between streets near the town square.

Dumitra found me leaning against the paddock fence. She spat out some herbs she had chewed and mixed them with water in a bowl.

"Here." She took the wad and placed it over my swollen eye. "This will help with the swelling and bleeding. Mama Tudora has taught me well. Hold this in place as you watch your sheep. Now I must tend to mine." And off she ran.

The night became rowdy with music, food, and much drunkenness. The sheep shifted and bleated in their tight space. Petra and I lay down on the hay piled next to our corral. I decided I had never been safer with my flock and soon floated into slumber. As I nodded, someone grabbed my collar and shook me.

"Wake up!" Dumitra shook me from my slumber.

"What? What?" I was groggy from sleep.

"While you may think all the wolves are outside of these walls, you are wrong." She pointed towards Lancu and some other large boys smiling and standing next to a nearby wall.

Lancu had a rock he was playfully tossing in the air and catching in his hand. He sneered in my direction. His long dark hair fell out from under his felt hat like the reflection of a river at night. Then he pointed in my direction and they began to move closer. With rabbit quickness, Dumitra pulled an arrow from her quiver, drew back, and aimed.

The boys all stopped in a dusty skid. "She's the one that never misses," said one of the boys with a shaky voice.

"It's true," said another.

Lancu laughed hideously. "Now he has a girl to protect him. Can he not fight?"

I stood. "I can fight. You may see. But, I say this," I hesitated and blew out air with, "Let us be friends."

Lancu sputtered as he laughed, "Someone has been listening to old Shepherd tales. Let us be friends- Paahhh!" The other boys joined in the frivolity.

I bounced down off the soft hay, "I say again—no truer words have I spoken—let us be friends." Tata would have been proud. I wondered in that instant—has Tata yet regained his health?

Lancu was vain and cocky. He seemed to like being the center of attention. "I will show you what. We will see how you fight in the Shepherd Contest; I do not think too well if you must rely on a girl to protect you." He sputtered laughter and a strand of drool snailed down his chin.

I kept my silent stance. Then Dumitra did something I wished she hadn't. She aimed and shot an arrow. It whizzed through the air and tore Lancu's hat from his head and pinned it against a wall behind. Lancu and his group froze silent.

"The next will be through your heart." Dumitra's sincerity could not be doubted.

Somewhat shaken, Lancu pulled the arrow from the wall and snapped its shaft over his knee. He put his hat back on with its new hole. Then, he and his companions ambled down the street into the shadows.

Dumitra ran and picked up the broken arrow and tip-toed back unwinding the sinew which held it to the shaft. "I saw your necklace. Can I add to it?" she asked. She stood close to me with one hand on my shoulder. With skilled hands, she used the sinew to secure the arrow to my necklace.

"Why do you give this to me?" I asked.

"You must know—you are my best friend." Her words made my heart flutter like a moth. "Someday I know you will be much more." I shuffled in the hay and my cheeks burned hot. I could not look straight at her. I kept silent. "You are tired, my best friend. Now go to sleep. I will watch over your sheep," she glowed with a slim confident grin.

I nodded and then stretched out on the hay. For some time I did not go to sleep. I held the arrow on my necklace in my hand knowing an angel stood near. It would always remind me love is my greatest protector and my greatest love would always be Dumitra. With the arrow in my hand, I drifted off to the most wonderful dream. When I finally woke, it was quiet. I noticed the sky already turning a hint of blue although the stars were still out. I stood up and yawned. "Dumitra, now it is time for you to get some sleep."

"Oh, it is too late. The market will be starting soon. My father will have a fire going. I will go and cook some food. Maybe you will be lucky and have an egg with some bread." She playfully bounced off seeming to have more energy than I.

I smiled and she smiled back. She jogged off as though she never grew tired—out of the town's gate and off to her flock on the hill.

***

I hold the arrow in my hand and press the smooth flint between my thumb and forefinger. Whenever I need to think more clearly, I do this. Since that night, this arrow has become a part of me. Without it, I do not know what I would do. It always reminds me of the greatest strength—love.

Dumitra is still as stubborn and strong, as the day she gave me this gift. I did not know where all this would lead, but she did. Always. She made me believe.

A cool wind blows in. Dumitra, Tata Grigore, and Mama Tudora sleep in the houses below. My decision will affect each of us. I hoped and prayed my choice would be the right one. Either way, I take a risk.

***

The town square was filled with hustle and bustle. Most were men from throughout the country areas (though I did pick out a few foreigners) in the morning light. Some wore traditional clothing and some wore the fancy garb of buyers. The Shepherds dressed always in plain cloaks as they served a simple function—warmth and protection.

I stood up and brushed the hay off my clothes. Carts and wagons rolled into town. I noted my eye had swollen further in the night and I barely had vision through the swollen slit of my puffy lid.

The sheep began moving restlessly and I threw some hay in with them. I took a nearby bucket and fill the trough. When I was finished, I saw Dumitra running in with something in her hands. She handed me a treat of eggs and a thick slice of bread.

"You are hungry. Doing a man's work makes you this way. My Tata will come soon to see your sheep sell as they should. He told me you must not leave his side after the buyer pays. We do not need bandits to run off with your family's profits." She gently patted my eye and kissed my forehead.

"Tell your Tata, thank you. I will do as he says."

My sheep went up for sale early. Several buyers bid and I admit I was content with their price. Before the auctioneer could end the sale though, Barbu stood up next to him. "You all know Grigore. He is a good man. He took ill and is in his bed at home. His adopted son has taken it upon himself to get these sheep to market. Let's show Grigore we care for him and his lovely wife. Let's bid as we should."

The whole town seemed to talk amongst themselves. Then the bidding grew and grew. Oh, I thought, Tata and Mama will be happy! The sheep sold for the highest price at the market. Afterward, people from the town approached me to express concern. Some, too, looked at me oddly saying, "I did not know Grigore and Tudora had another son. Why would they keep such a secret?"

I explained Grigore had found me nearly dead and Tudora had brought me to health. I kept to my lie of being a wandering orphan; it seemed enough to calm the questions. Some brought with them food like smoked meats and dried fruit. One even brought me a berry pie. I could not chase off the smile on my face. My parents would celebrate the profits and kind wishes.

After the auction, some sheep were off to the butcher's knife. Many more festivities unfolded with drummers, puppet shows, and minstrels. I saw so many things. Even animals from afar. Leopards on ropes and a monkey sat upon his Master's shoulder stealing food from passers-by. Dumitra explored the streets with me. She fed me cheese sandwiches from a sack she carried opposite her quiver.

Mr. Chatar was the primary speaker at the market festival. He was the assistant to the Burg and held great authority in the town. His hand was held high for the crowd to silence. "This afternoon will be the Shepherd Festival. Young Dumitra of the mountains will begin our festivities. She will show her prowess as an archer. None can match her skills. Then we will place the Shepherds against each other. They will have tests of strength and cunning—first will go the boys and then the men. Our competition begins with wrestling. Each match will end when one competitor sits upon the other. The second contest will be staff fighting." His eyes wandered from Shepherd to Shepherd. "Who has not had to fight off a wolf?"

Yells and loud laughter from the crowd made the street a joyful place. "You brave Shepherds will put your staff to use against another until a solid body hit. Of course, a broken staff, or a yell from your opponent will end the game. Do we understand the rules?" Chatar looked around the gathering.

"Da! Da!" The shouts from the crowd sent a flock of pigeons flying from the rooftops. "Then let us show our appreciation as fair Dumitra approaches to show us how a bow and arrow is mastered," suggested Chatar. Cheers came from everywhere and some heckles (I suspected from Lancu or his friends).

Dumitra stepped up onto the platform where earlier the auction had taken place. She bowed. "Sometimes I am bored watching my sheep and I set up targets to practice." She pulled an arrow from her quiver.

Barbu ran over nodding to let her know the targets were prepared. Each was a circle of wood and each smaller in size and at different distances on top of a high stone fence. The crowd watched with care. It was silent except for the sound of distant flocks.

"One," she shouted as her first arrow whizzed swiftly and solidly toward the first target. Twang! It cracked as it hit the mark. "Two," another arrow was off as quickly and hit the next target. "And, three!" she shouted as the third arrow took flight and flew to the third target hitting it at dead center. The audience cheered and applauded.

"Now I will shoot moving targets. Since no birds are in flight, my Tata will throw some old tavern plates far above your heads. Watch!" Barbu looked at her and she nodded. He had three aged chipped plates which he threw high, higher, and highest. Quick from her quiver came the arrows—one, two, three! Dumitra's arrows flew straight and true. One plate fell. The second plate fell and, finally, the third plate shattered. The crowd roared with approval. Dumitra smiled gently and bowed again before stepping down from the platform. Halfway down, she spotted me and wandered in my direction.

Mr. Chatar returned to the platform, the stairs bent down with each step. He stood a moment and then waved the crowd to silence. "Now, we will begin the boys' wrestling. All boys participating come up here

Dracula's Son

now." His finger made a line outlining the platform. I stood for a second. I decided I would not take part.

From behind came a push. It was Dumitra. "Well. Voicu, how else can we know how you fare? I will be watching. You may not be the biggest, but I do know you have some fight in you." So, I had no choice, I stepped forward.

I was among a dozen or so boys of various sizes. Lancu stood on the opposite end of the line. I looked down to see his teeth shining back in an awful expression.

"We will not do the wrestling or staff fighting here. A well-used pig sty on the other end of the Market Square has always served best and should make all the falls less rough, although dirty," explained Chatar.

The crowd parted as we kept in our line, marched over, and stood to one side of the messy pen. Chatar waddled along making his way alongside the pen.

I waited not knowing what came next. Then Chatar directed two of the bigger boy to begin. They threw each other side to side. Cheers and hoots were echoing across the square. They grabbed each other around the waist. They did a sloppy kind of muddied dance and soon fell over. The shouting rose. As one grabbed the other's ear and the other grabbed his opponent's hair in return; the fighting got nasty. They kicked and scuttled about. One tried to stand and the other pulled him down with a wham! The lad was sitting on top of the other in a flash. That hurt! The people laughed, roared and some even snorted. Oh, it was merry!

The winner stood tall and proud scanning the waiting boys to pick his next opponent. He wandered down the row and stood in front of Lancu with a slight nod. The losing boy stomped out in silent shadows.

Lancu jumped into the pen giving the winning boy no time to recover. Without hesitation, he picked up some pig manure and slopped it into the winner's face. Trying to clear his eyes of the stuff, Lancu swiftly ran around and into the boy's backside. As Lancu hit the boy full-on, he made a loud grunt. Lancu sat on top of the struggling boy. It happened so fast as to make me wonder whether it had been rehearsed.

Mr. Chatar declared his son the winner. The competition went on each time getting nastier. Lancu was willing to do anything of mean and unfair play to win. It seemed only winning counted, to him. He took down several more boys.

Then he looked in my direction beckoning me into the pen. I handed Dumitra my cloak and Barbu my money bag. I did not know what to expect. Though he was winded, he seemed ready and was a full head's height above me in size. I stood tense and ready for the fight. He charged and I veered right as he fell sliding full force into the mud. The crowd cheered and I, mistakenly, smiled at him. His anger welled up as he rose and, with bloodshot eyes, like a bull he rammed towards me full force. This time, I was not so quick. He hooked an arm around my neck and punched me in my injured eye. I dropped face down in pain. Then I felt his full body weight drop on me like a boulder from above. My body crackled, as he sat solidly on me. The crowd cheer was difficult to hear, as I fought to get a clear breath. He kicked more mud in my face and he coolly pranced away.

"We have a clear winner—my son, Lancu. He's not one to fight lightly!" announced Mr. Chatar.

As I stumbled out feeling some body pains, but sorer in my pride, the crowd cheered. Lancu was soon declared the overall winner of the game.

Next, the men took to the pig sty; it was less mean and more fun. One man comically ran around in circles after Barbu had picked him as an opponent. I washed my face in a nearby bucket, as the crowd's laughter echoed through the streets.

Dumitra came and helped me to clean my wound. "We will not have this get infected," she declared. "It was not your event. He is bigger and stronger. You will do your best in the staff fight. I have seen you

Dracula's Son

use it against the wolves. I will wash your cut and you will soon be ready." My wound stopped bleeding and swelled further.

Mr. Chatar was again up front. "Barbu Straten, once again you have shown your fierceness. Once again, we ask- is he more man or bear?" The crowd laughed and some started a growl which grew into claps and roars. Barbu raised his hands high and mimicked the claws of a bear.

"Your father fights well," I submitted.

"Of course, he does. How else could he deal with my Mama?" Dumitra explained. The brow over my good eye rose in response. "The bleeding has stopped. Can you see well enough?" she asked.

"Yes." I had a sudden surge of energy. Then I took my staff and wandered to a nearby alleyway empty except for a pair of kittens chewing on some fish bones. I swirled and twirled it—twisting it from side to side. Remembering all the techniques I had learned with a sword so long ago. All the lessons on attacks and thrust and blocking came back. Thank you, Sir Stephan. Even with only one good eye, I felt well-prepared.

"Boys' staff battle. Boys come up front," Mr. Chatar announced standing in front of the pig sty. He looked surprised to see me hurry through the crowd and step forward to join the line.

I guess my eye was quite ugly by this time. Some in the crowd, especially the women, pointed and shook their heads. "Why he should not be allowed in the pen," one said. "He has only one eye to use," said another. I stood tall up front and waited.

Several of the bigger boys started. They fought well but slowly – soon one fell and the battle was won.

After several rounds of fighting, Lancu was selected. He stepped into the pen. I watched his style. His moves were sharp and crisp. For such a big boy, he could move quickly. Soon he had the other boy down and was declared the winner. It looked like it could be a repeat of the wrestling match.

I must have looked like an easy target. Lancu glared at me and smilingly mocked me into the pen. I stepped in and brushed my hand against the smooth of my staff. My focus of energy and eye was singly determined. I would fight my very best. I looked him straight on, without dropping my eyes in the least or showing any emotion.

He came forward quickly and our staff clacked. Back and forth, we parried. At first, I acted to defend myself, and then I saw he was growing tired. I put on a full battle. I clicked hitting him hard in the side. I swirled again whacking against his head and making him bleed. With my final swirl, I hit behind his knees causing him to fall backward into the mud. The crowd's cheer was deafening! He did not get up for some time. Another boy ran in with a bucket of water and splashed it on his face. I won. The two remaining boys bowed out and I was declared the winner for staff fighting.

Lancu stood to the side, not looking back my way. His pride was hurt and so was his body. He would think twice before trying to fight me again in the future. But it was clear, that he considered me an enemy.

"The winner of the boy's staff fighting is Voicu, son of Grigore. Though many agree I am certain he need only have hit the fighter Lancu once to have won." Mr. Chatar looked the other way and stepped down the platform to check on his son.

Dumitra came up and gave me a happy slap on the shoulder. "I knew you could do it! And with such style! You were fantastic!"

We skipped together to the gate and outside. Petra sat chewing on a bone he had found somewhere. He got up and carried the bone off to some secret place as he noticed our approach. It was starting to get late.

Barbu came up behind us and handed me my money sack. "It is best if we start now. We will stay together. Most of the bandits will not expect those with money to leave until tomorrow. Their prowling will start early in the morn. Somehow, they think shepherd folk are as lazy as they!" He laughed as we stepped into the darkness.

Our hike back up the mountain was much quicker without sheep. I admit I had a difficult time keeping up with Dumitra and Barbu. Eventually, Petra caught our scent and found us in the climbing hills.

"Oya! Oya! Oya!" cried out Dumitra as we approached the house early in the next morning's light. When we arrived, Mama and Tata were up drinking some tea and they gave each of us kisses on the cheeks. I relaxed seeing Tata so well.

Barbu and Tata wandered off in conversation. Mama made Dumitra and I sit to eat pastries and porridge. She must have expected our arrival.

Tata looked well, but he coughed now and then which gave me some concern. When he and Barbu returned, I handed him the money sack. Oh, Mama danced about as she peeked over his shoulder. She said, "I have never seen so much money."

I also emptied my other sack of dried fruit and sausages. Then, I shared about my winning the staff fight.

"Yes, but it looks like you paid the price." Tata touched my swollen eye. We visited until late at night. Finally, Barbu rose to leave. I went outside and, under the stars, Dumitra gave me a sweet kiss. I kissed her back—not on her cheek, but her lips. She may have blushed as she skipped off. I could not tell. I held the cold arrow around my neck as she disappeared into the woods. We, each of us, slept with peace, contentment, and exhaustion. I was sore but in a very good way.

Chapter 10

Skinny Sheep

Sheep bleats rise with the sun and I know I must return soon. Our flock is sickly and few but, as Tata says, I must be thankful for all I have. I am a rich man! But, now I must make a choice. I know clarity will come. Yes, clarity will come.

***

The next year, Mama and Tata sat me down with, "Soon you will want to leave. Maybe this year? Maybe next? You must not worry about us," Tata stated. Mama nodded in agreement. Every night I would kiss the arrow around my neck and wonder when I would see Dumitra again. It seemed I was always thinking of her. She often visited my dreams and I waited impatiently for our time together. I grew taller, my voice deepened, and hair sprouted on my face and other places unmentionable.

Word spread in the hills of a meeting for an Easter celebration. A priest made the long journey from the nearest monastery. He arrived at one of the mountain homes and that is where the locals met. Tata insisted that I go with Mama to this event; he would stay behind and tend the sheep. Mama wandered off with other women almost the instant we arrived at the event. I found myself alone until I heard a sweet voice.

"Oya! Oya! Oya!" She skipped through the flowery meadow like a wood nymph about to cast a spell.

"Dumitra you have come to celebrate." I contained my excitement. "It is good. How is your family?" She was silent. "Do you know it may rain later? Have you gathered the wool from your sheep?" I stuttered trying not to turn red.

"Oh, you—always with the same questions. Why don't you ask how I am doing?"

I cleared my throat, "How are you doing?"

She looked at me curiously and stepped forward. "I am fine," she said with another step towards me, "now."

My thoughts muddied. "Good," crackled a sound from my throat. Was that my voice?

"Can we go for a walk?" she asked.

"Dumitra, he needs a walk. I give you my blessing," said Mama Tudora. Where did Mama come from? "The celebration starts midday, so you may take him." Mama Tudora nodded low as the women standing behind her giggled. How did they all sneak up on us?

Side by side, we hurried from the mother hens and away from big eyes. Once we were away from others, she brushed her hand against mine. My thoughts went in every direction like a murder of crows taking flight. Her fingers found mine and then we twined them together. We spoke and laughed, but I cannot recall a single word. Her grip was tight and caused me to feel tingles and flames all over my body. We hiked to the hilltop and back. Our hands parted as we approached the circle of women waiting with smiles.

Too quickly the Easter celebration came to an end, Dumitra waved goodbye and I took the long journey home with Mama.

"Dumitra is a good young lady," Mama stated with a smile.

"Yes, she is," I agreed.

Mama stopped me for a moment and focused on my reaction. "I like her. She comes from a good family and she is pretty," Mama had a twinkle in her eye.

I stammered, "Yes, Mama, she is pretty."

"And you are handsome," Mama patted my arm and winked, "Ah, maybe one day?"

***

Shortly after the Easter celebration, I sat one evening on the fence of the corral. I watched the sun slowly fall and the sky turn the color of flowers and melon's inside. The wind shifted and bits of sand and dirt found their way into my mouth. I spit. She was on my mind. I missed her already.

"Son, you are in a thought trap?" Tata leaned against a post.

"I'm wondering if we will be going to the market this summer."

"The market—this is what's on your mind? Hmmm," he stroked his chin, "Yes, we will go to the market. We haven't so many to sell this year, but we will take some." Tata cleared his throat. "The flock is small enough for just one shepherd. Maybe you would rather stay behind. I can go on my own."

"No. No. I will go just in case there is some unpredictable happening," I said.

"Oh, you are a good son! Well, if you feel you must," Tata smiled.

I will see Dumitra again at the market. My body filled with calm warmth and my lips formed an easy smile. The time would be as a turtle but soon we would be together again!

Tata hesitated. "There is something else I want to talk to you about." He looked off towards the horizon. "You are becoming a man. It is a big responsibility and one which will complete your life. Though you are not quite ready, soon you will want to start your flock."

"Yes, Tata, I suppose I will, but, for now, I will help with your flock," I said.

He took my hand and patted it with the other. The creases below his eyes mimicked the curve of his smile. "This is not the flock I am talking about. I mean children—a wife and family. God made it such. We need this."

I nodded in agreement trying not to blush.

"Mama is so happy with the thought. I'll leave you now. If you have any questions, Voicu, any questions at all, please ask me." Tata shuffled off into the woods whistling as he carried a bucket to fetch water from the stream.

This was the season I truly felt I had become a Shepherd. Sometimes, Tata and I watched the flock together—sometimes I watched the flock alone. I felt like I was becoming part of the mountain and nature and a family. I felt like a man or a holy monk finding balance in the still-cool mountain air. I enjoyed the times I had with Mama and Tata at our simple home. I also found contentment in my time alone on the mountain.

Many were the nights I stayed awake and watched over the flock in the hills and the mountain pasture. As the sheep settled in the pale purple lights of dusk, I would find a place to sit. The beauty of the light and shadows of the mountains and forest. I breathed deeply the pine scent and smiled. I searched the dark blue of the sky for the single light of the night's first star. Sometimes Petra was not enough company. I found myself reaching under the itch of my shirt for the smooth flint of the arrow. She was out there somewhere. And the medallion, I held this too. The ram image memorized by the touch of my thumb always led to a silent prayer of thanks for Mama and Tata. I was never alone.

The time went by like the moon rolling across the sky. It wasn't once or twice each day that I thought about Dumitra; it was constant and unending. I would picture her and I was certain she was picturing me. I prayed that God would make the time go quicker or that I would have more patience. Tata slept on the far side of the flock, trusting I was watching. I could see the lump of his body on a small hillock below.

Petra wandered around the sheep scanning off into the forest. Dogs do understand the wild better that people. Petra circled here and there until content, then came and to lie next to me.

"Everything is safe?" I tossed pebbles against the trunk of high mountain pine. Petra looked up at me waiting for a pet behind the ear. "Good—such a good dog. Can I talk to you Petra?" I lowered myself down next to him. He rolled over exposing his belly while keeping one eye on the sheep. "I'm in love with her and I don't know what to do. I can't stop my mind from thinking about her. It makes me crazy. Four more days and I'll see her. Oh, I wish she was here right now. I would hold her hand." Petra made some small growl and then was up and chasing off some shadow. "I would tell her I love her," I shouted as he rushed into some nearby shrubs in chase of some swift-footed rabbit.

***

In several days we drove the flock down to the corral and separated those for the market. Mama watched us leave and I must have taken off more quickly than usual as Tata said, "Slow down, Son. The market will not start for several days. Let us enjoy the walk down. We do not need to hurry to Arefu." Tata whistled some cheerful tune and barely on our way he suggested, "Remember the pond beyond the trees? Let's stop for a swim and to wash up. We have so much time and why miss such a chance?"

We swam and scrubbed our arms and legs with the rough of some rushes. "Voicu would you go get some apples from my satchel? I will just lay and dry in the sun, then I would like a little smoke. Maybe even a short nap. I am getting older, you know."

"Yes, Tata," I dragged myself out of the water and then returned with his pipe.

"Oh, such a pleasant day!" Tata bit into his apple. He reclined across the rock and soon appeared to be sound asleep.

What is wrong with Tata? I asked myself. Finally, I shook him awake. "Oh, Voicu, I was having such a nice nap. Well, I suppose we should get the sheep on their way." He rose with a stretch and yawn. So unlike Tata. Maybe age truly is starting to slow him?

Did I go faster than usual? I couldn't tell. At every turn of our path, Tata had some reason to pause. "Oh, God has given us a beautiful day." Or "Let's stop and collect some mushrooms." Or "Stay and watch the sheep. I will catch a rabbit to roast tonight."

The days we journeyed seemed longer than the whole season! I did not want to wait. She was close. When I lay down, my eyes were like window shutters unsettled in a restless wind. What little sleep came was with the sweetest of thoughts.

On the third and longest of days, the meadows opened to a far-off view of the town walls. Flocks everywhere, I scanned the crowd for Dumitra. There she was! I waved but she must not have seen me.

"I will go to make arrangements. Watch the sheep, Voicu." Tata wandered off towards the crowd. While I scanned over our small flock, I could see Tata stopping to talk to almost everyone along the way. He ambled along to see a friend here and a friend there—and never a simple hello. At each stop, as he tottered like some old street beggar towards the gate, it seemed he visited every single person along the way. Why did he take so long? I lost sight of Dumitra. She must have been beyond the gates. I held the arrow in one hand and my staff in the other. My eyes grew tired of watching Tata's slow business.

The sheep grazed along the slope. Petra inched up to me and dropped with a Hummpphhh! His head on my feet looked up and his eyes said, Relax. Sit down and scratch behind my ears. We are in no hurry. "Even you would slow my pace. Even you, my faithful dog!"

With my mind, I tried to beckon Dumitra to us, but it did not work. Then the smallest thought began—maybe she does not want to see me. Why I would think this, I do not know, but I did. And then it happened. A pebble bounced off my backside. At first, I thought I must be mistaken. I looked back across the flock and down to the swarm of people like ants from a broken mound. Pop! A clump of dirt powdered my shoulder.

I turned around and scanned the forest and the field with eyes weighted with dust and sleep. There was nothing. Petra stood alongside me and sniffed the air. He lowered close to the ground and glided across the grass towards a bush on the hillside.

"Oya!" Dumitra jumped up like a rabbit scared from its den.

I steadied myself with my staff. "Oh, it is a fox! Good Petra bring me its pelt!"

She bounded down the hill with laughter.

I hurriedly put the arrowhead back under my shirt.

"It is good that I was not out to hunt you. I would already have you on a spit over my fire." She came up close to me. Her eyes pulled me in. Then her smell made me sway.

As though planned, Tata's came up the hill a moment later. "I told you to watch the sheep—not the pretty girls that go by."

I couldn't speak. My head turned from Dumitra to Tata to Dumitra and back. My mouth moved but I could not form words.

"I will take over now. Would you please watch over that pretty girl and protect her. She wants to go into town for a walk," Tata said.

Dumitra brushed against me as she passed. "I want to go now. Let's not wait until the sheep settle!"

Tata's eyebrows rose as he patted me on my shoulder, "That is a woman who knows what she wants."

"Voicu will be back to give you a break before nightfall," Dumitra explained to Tata. "Come, Voicu. We haven't all day." Tata laughed as he leaned against his staff.

We stepped in silence. My hand twitched like a spider about to secure a fly stuck in its web, as I anticipated touching her hand. Once we were hidden within the crowd, it happened. Gentle like a butterfly's wings her hand brushed against mine, then we each clasped.

"Did you miss me?" Dumitra swung our hands as she turned towards me. I kept to her eyes and tried not to inspect the way her body was developing.

"I thought about you some." I took a deep breath out.

"Just some?"

My heart raced but I could not say the words. "More than some." I stuttered.

She stopped me and pulled me onto a quiet side street. Holding both of my hands she looked straight into my eyes. "Voicu, speak plainly."

"I…I…I…" I took a deep breath and focused on her. What are the words I want to say?

"Out of my way peasant boy!" Lancu stepped out of the shadows catching me off guard and pushing me away from Dumitra.

My anger felt like a pot of stew about to boil over and burn anyone in its way. "Why did you do that?" I straightened myself and brushed it off. Dumitra stood by my side.

"Do I need a reason?" Lancu had two armed soldiers standing behind him.

Then I noticed the official garb he wore. Was he working for the Prince? I breathed in deeply and let my anger melt away.

"Speak up! I want to hear what a Shepherd has to say." Lancu stepped toward me.

He had pushed me away from my love. I wanted so to push him back but knew it was not wise. I pictured competing with him on the morrow. Yes, I would have my revenge but on my terms. I smiled and took one more deep breath, "let us be friends."

"His words are as weak as he is." Lancu's guards laughed at his jest as they marched off.

Dumitra stood quiet like some magical tree turned into a woman. The wind sucked down the alley and blew her hair into her face and she pulled it aside. "Why is it you speak kinder to Lancu than me?" I went to take her hand and she pushed it away. "I will leave you alone to find the words you have to say to me. If they are the right ones, then we will go for another walk. Look for me after the games tomorrow. Until then, I walk on my own." She swayed away and, as she turned onto the street, side glanced back to see my reaction.

I was stunned. I blinked and dumbly blinked again. What has just happened? Lancu had ruined everything. I was about to say what I wanted to say. What I had thought about saying. I love you. I wanted to find Lancu and end this frustration. I breathed deeply. Tomorrow, I thought, I will get my revenge.

My face flushed making the cool of dusk feel even cooler. I was quick to navigate the crowd out through the main gates and back up the hill.

Tata leaned against his staff. "Voicu, you come back early. Why would you leave such a pretty girl?"

"She left me," I said.

Tata put his hand on my shoulder. "I want you to tell me what happened. Tell me what went wrong."

Dracula's Son

"It is complicated," I let out the air in a huff.

"Yes, women are. But what happened?" Tata gripped my shoulder and watched my eyes to read them.

"She said she wanted to walk alone," I tried not to let a tear form, but one did. I hoped he did not see. I brushed it away.

"That's all? That's not so bad," Tata shared.

"Iancu was there. He pushed me."

"Did you push back?" asked Tata.

"No, but I wanted to," I kicked a rock and watched it roll down the slope.

"Voicu, it would solve nothing. You would be showing him that he has more power over you than you do yourself." Tata turned away from the flock. "What will you do?"

"Tomorrow at the games I will show Iancu how I push."

"Good, Son. Let your anger out in the sport. Others will see it as competition. Whatever happens though, do not let him control your anger. Always you must forgive." He squeezed my shoulder, "Let's get these sheep within a fence."

***

The auction and sheep sales went quickly. From where I stood I could see Dumitra; our eyes met for only an instance. I would have to win her love and attention back. I would have to beat Iancu in the Shepherd games.

"Mama will be happy with the money we bring back." Tata held the money pouch up for me to see. "We will have some time to shop before we leave. Maybe I will get a gift for Mama?"

"You are already spending your money?" Barbu parted the crowd to join us, "Be careful!"

"What else is it for?" Tata put his hands in the air to exaggerate his point.

"Shhh! Chatar is climbing back up on the stage." Barbu put his giant hand over Tata's mouth.

"The Shepherd's games will start shortly. I know it will disappoint many, especially you young ladies. My son has moved beyond boyhood games. His appointed position requires him to stay in uniform. He will, yet, have an announcement from the Prince after the games are over. Without any more words let us be off to the pig sty." The crowd shifted toward the other side of town. My disappointment must have shown.

"You will not be able to sport with Lancu. I know this must frustrate you. God must have a plan. In the end, it is always that good wins...not evil. This will always be so. Do not doubt that, Son." Tata put his arm over my shoulder as we wandered over toward the pigsty. "I still expect you to compete. And, of course, you will win."

I won both in wrestling and staff fighting but felt little satisfaction. I guess much of what I had meant to use against Lancu, I used against others. One had a broken hand and another a swelled eye. I managed through the whole affair to not suffer injury.

As I dripped off pig manure and sweat, Lancu approached his father.

"Are the boys done with their games?" He sneered down from the high platform. Was he looking at me?

Chatar raised his hand for silence. "My son has some words to share. Please give him your attention."

"The Prince does send greetings. I have recently accepted an appointment with him. I will speak more on these matters at dusk. No one will leave the township until after this important message." The guards around the base of the stage shuffled into position. Lancu was certainly on a less diplomatic and more forceful mission. He stepped down and it was then that everyone began to notice the number of soldiers present. Several lines stood guard at the gates. Something strange was unfolding.

Dumitra took my hand in full view of everyone present. Letting go she approached a nearby trough then hoisted a bucket of water and splashed it on my face. "You cannot smell of pig while you walk with me. The words you have for me cannot wait."

We strolled through the streets and the market. The smells of faraway fragrances and beautiful fabrics of the finest make filled the stalls. I felt like I was in a dream as we wandered up and down the streets and around the market square.

"Maybe someday I will be your queen." Dumitra held up some fabric over her mouth. Then she looked back behind me.

"What are you looking at?"

"I fear we are being followed my king."

I turned back to see Barbu and Grigore quickly turn away. "Have they been following us long?"

"Oh, yes. They have been watching us from a distance all day. Someday I must teach you to hunt."

"Do you care to lose them?" I asked.

"They are both swift and strong. I do not know if it is possible." Dumitra giggled and dropped the fabric back to the table.

"But we together are such a good team," I shared. "I have a plan. I will rush across the square, down the narrow road, and wait behind the church. You will take the street behind and go around and over."

"You are also wise." She instantly took off in full stride like a deer spooked by a hunter.

I strode towards the other side of the square and did not look to see Tata and Barbu's reactions. Then I took off like a thief with a farmer's piglet. When I made the corner behind the church, I was breathless. Dumitra stood calm and composed waiting.

"We have lost the spies." She took my hands and pulled me closer.

"Yes." I panted as I tried to stand tall. "And now I have something I must say to you. I have wanted to speak these words for some time."

"I am listening."

My heart pounded like the hoof beats of a wagon horse set free in the pasture. My mouth was dry—where is my spit? Am I close or far? I lost my senses in her eyes. "I...I...I love you." Her body came to mine. The softness of her breast and hips pressed against me as she hugged me tightly. Her warm breath floated across my neck and cheek. "Voicu, I love you too."

I forgot about the time. Our lips touched as her fingers twirled up and down my arm. I swear I had fallen from some high cliff and sprouted wings mid-flight! Together we were like some smaller version of the church steeple in whose shadow we stood.

Suddenly, there was a great move as the people mimicked the sheep crowding the town square. We wandered in behind the crowd—happy, content, silently our hands held us together as one. Lancu stood on the platform and raised his hand for silence. Several dozen soldiers stood in lines around the base.

"As you good citizens know, I am now in the service of the Prince of Wallenchia. He has asked me to inform all the shepherds they need to be legal in their financial transactions. I am here as the Prince's Official to tell you, that you must pay your taxes. One-tenth of your total is a fair amount and it will be collected here and now. This is the end of illegal profits! Pay as you leave or suffer the consequences." A quick shuffle and more soldiers came in to protect Lancu. The gates were heavily guarded. Men shouted showing their displeasure. A sea of soldiers with swords drawn waited to assist in the collection and surrounded the crowd. Lancu is the appointed tax collector! I could not believe the injustice! Dumitra and I moved up behind our Tatas and I felt confused.

"What has this become?" Barbu shook his head as he turned to Tata Grigore. Tata responded, "I do not understand such a tax. It looks as though we will have no choice. I will not leave my wife a widow and without a son. We will pay and leave." I followed in the wind behind his cloak. My hand slipped from hers as I glanced back. When will I see Dumitra again? And, so we left with far much less than we expected from our efforts. Into the night, we hiked. After a short rest in the depth of night, our steps beat a steady pace. Through the forest shadows caused by the full moon, Tata kept a pleasant smile. My legs ached as we rounded onto a familiar path. The chimney smoke from the house ahead made my stomach growl in anticipation. When we arrived at the house, Tata went in to explain matters to Mama. I sat and watched the sheep wander around the corral and petted Petra.

In the time it took to check on the water and the yearlings, Tata's smile greeted me. "Voicu, Mama, and I have some work to do and I am concerned." Mama stood next to Tata with her mouth closed, arms folded and head nodding. "The sheep left in our corral still look skinny." I didn't agree but listened completely.

"The winter weather is still some time off. It would be best to take them up to the high mountain pasture for one week. I trust you will handle this well." Tata grabbed my shoulder with his strong clasp.

"Yes, Tata. When?"

"Tomorrow morning. Get some rest tonight and then you should be at the high pasture by midday."

"You do not want to come?" I asked.

"No, no, no. Mama and I have some matters to keep us busy. It is a small enough flock for you and Petra to watch over."

I nodded with a smile. Yes, Mama and Tata deserve some time alone. Mama nodded in agreement from her spot.

I slept soundly and woke to notice the arrow impression when I loosened my grip. Up to leave before the sun, Mama sat waiting at the table with a food bundle.

"Did you fill my bundle with rocks? It is heavy."

"No. You are a growing young man. You will need plenty to eat." It was odd for Mama to be so quiet and short of words. "Now you must get on your way," she said nearly pushing me out the door. Giving me a hug and a kiss, she and Tata waved me on my way. They seemed so excited about their time alone.

Petra and I took the sack and herded the small flock through the forest. The young sometimes trailed behind but quickly moved at Petra's prodding. Our slow trek did not bother me as the sunlight spilled into the forest and meadows. It made my spirit light and joyful. I sang a tune as I guided the sheep along moving close to our destination. Lost in thought about the starry nights, for some reason I reached for the arrow around my neck. Then I heard a noise. Was it a wolf? Did my ears play tricks on me?

"Oya! Oya! Oya!"

At first, I thought I must be mistaken, and then it came again more clearly.

"Oya! Oya! Oya!" It was Dumitra! She sat in the open field looking down at us as we stepped out from the forest.

"Voicu, why are you here?" She threw her arms up high with a smile from her high perch, then she bound down the hill.

"Tata told me to go and fatten these sheep for another week."

"This is the same thing my Tata said. 'Dumitra, these sheep left in the corral look skinny. Take them for a week to fatten.' Ha! This is why our Tatas have been talking and watching over us."

I laughed and then I looked at Dumitra. I thought of how beautiful she was. I could barely breathe. She stood perfect as the setting sun sent shadows across her face and chest. My angel. My love.

"Why do you look at me so?" She jumped down next to me.

An uncontrollable smile overtook my face as I offered my hand to her. "Will you go for a walk with me?"

We held each other's hands and, as we circled our combined flock, we laughed so fully and could not stop talking. The minutes became hours and soon it was late. We sat together on a log fallen near the forest edge. I felt such contentment. My heart played its song. The moment was a treasure.

"It is late, Voicu. Why don't you get some rest?" She put her hand on my thigh.

"Late, yes, but I cannot sleep." I pulled her close and gave her the softest kiss on her ripe lips.

She pulled her body close and we came together like the wind and a storm. My fingers followed the line of her spine with the bump, bump, and bump of her vertebra. Then, we held each other's hands tight and lay down together for some time. How had the sky filled with stars? It was as though God had spilled them from an open hand.

We watched the sheep in turns. She offered her lap as a pillow for my head and I accepted. After some time, I sat up again and she napped while I watched.

"What will become of us?" Dumitra stared into my eyes. Does she search my soul?

"We will be married, have children, and never worry about the wolves again," I explained with a laugh. Life is so very good!

"Sometimes Voicu you amaze me. Other times I am frightened a little when I look into your eyes. It is like a demon hides. Can you tell me, do you struggle?"

I looked back and then turned away. The stars were so far away. How can I ever tell her? "My struggle is my own. I suppose I am like every man, all I seek is love and peace."

"Love and peace you can have if you wish. But it will take more than you just saying these words." She rubbed my back and kissed the backside of my neck, "I do not want you to be lost. I want you to be here with me."

"Do you see the bright star? Tata Grigore told me it is called the Shepherd's Star. Of course, he told a story."

"I know the story well of the Shepherd who has lost his sheep. But then he realizes after wandering for so long, sometimes the flock must look for you. He sat and waited and somehow he became a bright star. The rest of the stars are his flock. My Tata has told me the same story. But why do you change the subject?"

"All are the Shepherd in one way or another. Flocks come and go in this life, but some stay. It's the ones that stay which are the greatest blessing." But, like Tata, she could look into my soul, and she said, "Someday you will tell me all."

And so the week went this way. During the day, we walked hand in hand and kissed and gathered flowers. At night, we sat up and talked and wondered. It was as though the universe was created for us—for our time together.

When it came time to sort the sheep and head home, we both shook with sadness saying our goodbyes. We held each other and squeezed with a kiss—as we pulled back our faces dripped with tears. I wanted to stay another day, another week, forever.

I wandered the mossy trails and grassy fields back home. I arrived to see an unexpected sight. Barbu and Tata were erecting a small house up the hill from Mama and Tata's. I must have looked confused as I opened the gate to the sheep corral.

"Where is she?" Mama ran up to me with a sweet smile.

I must have looked lost. "I do not understand."

"Why do you think we are building a home for you two?" Tata furrowed his brow. "My goodness! You mean to say in this whole week you had no time to ask for her to marry you?"

I laughed and felt a rush of blood on my face. "No. I…uh…no."

"Then it is time. You are both in love and have been for some time. Love is not something to send out to pasture, it is something to nurture." Tata's soft smile and kind eyes caused warmth deep inside of me. "Leave the sheep in the corral and find her. You cannot let it wait! Ask her, Voicu, to be your wife."

"But, we haven't a Priest." My cheeks warmed and my voice slightly trembled.

"In the mountains, you do not need a priest. You need only to ask her and God. It is then you are married." Tata put his arms around me and gave a kiss on each of my cheeks. "Honor her and she will honor you."

I herded the sheep in as quickly as I could. I hesitated none. "Yes. Yes, I will ask her to marry me." I fumbled and fell over a log. The group laughed.

To this Barbu nodded with a smile. "You have my blessing." He stepped close and lifted me with a hug which made my ribs feel weak and my breaths disappear.

I ran as never I have run before—up the hilly path of the mountain. I wondered if I would catch her before she had gone far. Later she would share her Uncle intercepted the flock so she could return. I stopped for a moment along the stream where the waterfalls and then in the distance, a voice rose. "Oya! Oya! Oya!"

"Dumitra!" I must have scared all of the birds for a mile.

"Yes, my love!"

"Will you?" I fumbled and my words came out odd.

"Yes, I will."

I stopped to catch my breath. "I mean," I stopped again and bent over to catch my breath, "will you marry me?"

She took my hand. "Yes, I said." Then she raised her voice and formally spoke to the Heavens. "I ask you and God to accept me as your wife, Voicu." Then she looked at me, "Well?"

"And, I ask you and God to accept me as your husband, Dumitra."

"I am your wife," she stepped forward.

"I am your husband," I pulled her close.

We kissed then forcefully and fully. Falling onto the bed of moss, we laughed.

Then I shook even so slightly, as she took my hand and placed it up under her blouse. My excitement was obvious. She kissed me and prompted me to assist in the removal of her clothes. Her dress dropped to the grass and reeds below. Then she helped me to remove my cloak.

We stepped into the water and under the falls. We held each other and it truly was as though I was with an angel. Alone, we were in paradise. The cool water falling eased my excitement, though not for long.

"You are my wife. Ha! Ha!" We looked into each other's eyes and some flutter of birds passed near our heads. In the afternoon sun, we were husband and wife for the very first time. It was a wonder and God truly smiled down upon us.

The day grew into darkness. We dressed and together, hand in hand, we followed the path back to our new home. The joy I felt made my mind wander and my body relax. I had such contentment. Nothing could change this, nothing except one thing—my past.

Chapter 11

Truth

I think about Dumitra. How would she take the news? Would she be angry? Would she be impressed? Would she think of me as capable of the evils of my father? Tonight, she is asleep in our bed alone. It is like we have been together forever, though it has only been a couple of years. And what of the coming winter? We might survive. Then there is our child Dumitra carries. If the babe is born near the winter's end, will Dumitra have the strength to deliver a healthy child?

I kick another pebble off into the ravine. A squirrel scampers up and down the nearby oak. Petra rearranges himself on our rock.

Then I think of Mama Tudora and Tata Grigore. They, too, would be disturbed knowing the truth. I stand in silence and take a deep breath of icy morning air. They are my parents now. They are my only parents. I do wonder about Tata. He has slowed since his illness long ago. Would he live if the illness strikes again?

And I have been here all night. And I have made my decision. I know what I must do. I will tell the truth. Yes, I will tell the truth. Even if it cost me my life, it could save my family. Now, I lay down for a short nap before I go to tell them my story. I am Dracula's son.

***

When I wake, the sun has already warmed the rock. Petra and I stumble down the slope toward home. We trudge slowly shuffling as we approach. Dumitra comes out the front door. "Here, my love." she hands me a cup of tea, hugs me, and kisses me on my lips. "I know you have had to make a big decision. I prayed God would guide you clearly—if it is to find labor afar or to sell the sheep or whatever it may be. I know it will be wise and I will trust."

"Thank you, my love. I have made my decision. Everyone must be here before I speak on this. It will affect all. It will not be easy, but I know what I must share. " I sip the tea and take my wife's hand, "All will be clear soon."

"I understand," she says and walks away in silence.

***

Tata left for the hills and will not return until nightfall. I tend to the posts of the corral; some have rotted and need replacement. It is quiet work and will calm my mind giving me time to think through my words. Dumitra and Mama set off to gather in the woods; they look weary even before they step out. I wave and place my hand over my heart as they go. They nod in my direction before they leave. They know, I tell myself, but how could they?

I collect new logs for post from the forest. It takes me most of the day. Petra stayed at the house and must be sleeping by the fire. My company is the squirrels and birds of the trees. My hands are cracked and sticky with pine sap from the day's work. As I drop the fresh post near the corral, the smell of some stew cooking comes from my parent's house.

Tata Grigore "Oya-A-Who!"s as he comes down the hill. I wipe sweat from my brow and wash my hands in the bucket of water near the door.

"Come, Voicu, let us eat." Tata puts his arm around my shoulder as we enter together. Mama and Dumitra set out the meager meal.

We sit for dinner together and eat a feast of rabbit stew and wild turnips. Soon our bellies are full. I am feeling relaxed until I think again of what

I must share. Then, we are all together and quiet, I must look deep in thought.

Tata turns to me. "Why does your face have such a serious look? We will recover the sheep. I know you have given this great consideration, son. Now may be the best time to tell us what you must."

"I am tired of thoughts and words going through my head," I pause gathering all of my concerns. "Last night, I was up fully until dawn thinking. Now I know what I must do." I put a log on top of the glowing embers. Our group of four gathers around the heat.

Mama Tudora shares, "Dumitra said she was worried about you and our dwindling flock. Yes, it will be a very hard winter without them. Yes, we may not even make it to spring. Never have I looked upon winter with so little." Mama Tudora holds her hands in prayer over her mouth and shakes her head back and forth slowly. She has tears already, "I worry too". How can I tell her the truth?

I take Mama's hand, "Yes, Mama. This is my concern too. But what I have to share here has not to do with sheep. It has to do with me." I stand and cannot help but shuffle my feet. "I have worries and concerns for us. I may be able to change matters for the better, but I risk making matters worse."

Tata raised one eyebrow and then turned to poke the fire, "Son, does this story have to do with finding you? I have always thought you hid something. I waited for you to share. Is now the time?"

"Yes." I begin with a deep breath, "I have not been honest with you". My eyes snake from one to the other in my family. "I have been living a lie. I am sorry," I pace from wall to wall and stop. "I followed the words of my true father. Some nine years ago he told me not to say who I was until I had safely made it across the border into Hungary. I escaped the Turks; this much is true. My mother jumped from the highest castle wall to the river below. I along with others escaped through a tunnel below the castle and planned to travel far. In the dark chaos, I fell from my father's horse to where you found me, Tata. You see, I am the son of Vlad Tepes, Dracula."

Mama Tudora giggles and pats me on the knee. "Oh, Voicu, such a story as this would have taken all night to think up. Why do you try to entertain us?"

The smoke from the fire dries my eyes as I look at Mama. I am silent. She saved me. We have been through so much together. My love for her and Tata is as great as this mountain we live on.

Dumitra looks me straight in the eyes for a moment and quietly searches. She holds my hand. "He is telling the truth." Then she kisses my hand and says, "Oh, my poor love. This is what has burdened you for so long."

"Please, Voicu." Tata Grigore turns on his knees in front of the hearth. Another log goes on the fire. "I did not find you in the clothing of royalty. You were in the clothes of a peasant. And the horses were not heading towards Hungary; they were heading towards the castle."

"I was dressed as a peasant should the Turks or others find me. The horses were shoed backward to confuse the Turks. If they saw the prints, they too would think we were heading towards the castle." Then I stop for a moment and breathe deeply as I hang my head. "I have proof. It is not what I wish to share, but I must." I took the medallion out from under my shirt and held the metal up and the light of the fire flickers off the shine of the proud ram. Oh, how I wish there was another way. "This is not the first like this I have seen."

Mama looks shocked and I know she now believes, "No, Voicu, no!"

"Yes." I pause thinking back with eyes sagging from a well of tears. "I saw your true son." I weep and my shoulders bounce up and down as I wipe the tears from my eyes. I must gather my voice through my own weeping though it will pain all, "It was my twelfth birthday. My father decided to give me strength. He took me to where he had people tortured. Those he would put up on poles. In the line was your son. He offered me the medallion before he was killed. I was to choose one person to live—my father's way of showing me I had power. Your son would not let me choose him. Oh, he was brave. And he smiled as he asked me to pick the woman behind. She was fat with babe."

"Did she live?" Grigore stands at his full height shouting and shaking me. It is the first time I felt fear of Tata. His voice rattled the rafters. "Tell me, Voicu, did she live?"

I sob barely able to say the words. "No. I chose her too, but my father told me it was cheating. He said I must choose her or her baby. I chose her and he put the sword through her babe."

Tata went and held Mama against his chest.

"Oh, the monster!" Mama's blouse soaks with tears. "The monster!" She and Tata stumble hand in hand out into the dark. They hold each other. They have aged years in only one night. I have pained them much!

Dumitra sits down next to me and puts her arms around me. "Oh, Voicu, if this is your real name, I do not know if life is crueler for the poor or those who rule. It is not a decision you should ever have needed to make. I am still your wife and this will always be. If you must travel through the gates of Hell, then so must I."

I think of how much I love my wife. I smell her hair as she draws me close. She wipes the tears from my eyes and off my face with her small hands. We hold our bodies close and I feel the sharpness of her rib cage. Have I grown weak with love?

"I must go to him," I say as I stand. "It is the only way." I see my reflection in the pools of my wife's eyes. I pull her close and we taste the salt of each other's tears as we kiss.

She silently stands holding my hands and her eyes cut into me like one of her arrows sharp and piercing. I dread her words. "Then so must I."

Dracula's Son

We sit in silence until the logs burn down to embers, and then Tata and Mama stepped back inside. Mama comes to me and kisses my cheek. "Grigore, talk to Voicu." Mama pushes him towards me.

He stood and looked at me with those eyes of strength. "I believe you fully. I know you have told me the truth. The woman behind my son was his wife. They were taken by soldiers when they went to visit the town. Your true father is cruel! I had thought one day I would like to impale him or his son in return. Now I have his son—and I call you my son. Why? Because, Voicu, he thought no more of you than to leave you to die in the wilds where I found you. God brought you to us because Dracula was without enough love for his own son. I know you will want to go to him. Maybe to explain you are still alive. I will not allow you to go alone. You are now my son. If he decides to kill you, he will first have to kill me."

"And I will go too." Mama takes Tata's hand and he looks at her with surprise.

"Voicu, you are not alone. We are a family. We must have faith that what unfolds, be it bad or good, happens as it should. "

"I wish that I could convince you to let me go on my own. But I know you too well. My father may be displeased that I am still alive. He may have me up on a spike to entertain his fancy. He may do the same to each of us. I do not know. My hope is he will let us live and grant a son's wish for food. This is what I pray for." I say a silent prayer of thanks and then kiss the cheek of Mama and Tata. To Dumitra I give a long kiss on the lips and do not hide my tears.

As a family, we decide to leave the next day. Barbu will come to visit in the morrow. He will want to join us. He will want to provide protection. Dumitra knows my thoughts. "Early in the morn, you must leave. I will speak to Tata Barbu. I will not lie. I will simply tell him that we have to journey. I do not wish for him to worry. I will tell him our explanation will come. He will take the sheep. After he leaves, I can follow your path and find you."

Mama Tudora is already packing what she can for our journey. "It will take us three days full and then some. We can hunt and cook along the way. God will provide." She looks at me. "Voicu." She pauses and I realize why.

"Mihnea. My true name is Mihnea."

"Mihnea, oh, Mihnea. It is so strange to call you by another name. Get some sleep. Tata and I will go to sleep soon. We have a long walk ahead of us."

I nod low and take Dumitra's hand as we step out into the cold.

"Mihnea. This is a good name," Dumitra kisses my cheek.

I feel light and though I could be filled with fear, I am not. I now know love. It is with me now. It is with me forever.

In the morning, we will begin.

***

The hike is long and strenuous. Mama surprises me and has no difficulty in keeping with our strides. Petra runs ahead marking trees here and there. Before we sit to eat dinner, Dumitra has caught up.

Each night Dumitra and I wander off holding hands and talking until we agree that we must go to sleep. Returning to the fire, we always find Mama and Tata close together soaking in the heat from the flames. None of us speak of what lies ahead. All our hearts are light until we come closer to our destination. The castle is only some hours away but we will stop for the night.

I think of the place and the memories. I was told the Turks had killed most left in the hold. The Sultan left the castle disappointed as my father was nowhere to be found. There may not be any other than my father who remembers me.

The weather is dull and wet. We huddle under our sheepskins and I help Tata to keep the flame of our fire from dying.

Dumitra runs up with a rabbit over her shoulder. "It is not much, but my arrow found its mark." She lays the buck down next to the circle. Petra whimpers. "Yes, there will be some for you." Petra drops at Dumitra's feet.

"Let us add these to the stew." Mama breaks a couple of wormy wild carrots and herbs.

"Ahead will be the river. The castle is up the flow and we will be there by midday. I do not know what will greet us. I must lead," I share. I look around the circle and all are silent.

Tata nods in agreement. "It is best this way. I will walk behind you with Mama."

Dumitra sets her quiver on the ground. "I have thought some on this. It may not be proper but I do not wish to walk behind you. I will be by your side. It is where I am most comforted."

For some reason this causes me to laugh, "I do not expect much comfort for any of us. If tomorrow is the last day on this earth, it would best be spent with you by my side."

None of us finds sleep that night. Even Petra is alert to every sound and movement from the trees. I am up in the drizzle and step into the water-heavy meadow. Though the sky is clouded over, the full moon breaks through sliced by a cloud knife.

Why have I brought those I love most here? I could have left on my own without speaking to them. My mind raced with thoughts. I can go there now. I can ask for a winter's stock of food. They would never have to go to the castle. I can be back before they wake. Yes, I will go.

I step along through the mud and find a stream leading to the river. Sore from snaps of low branches along the way, I am comforted by the sound of swift water ahead. It is the river. I step up onto the road which will lead up to the castle. The sound of something in a bush ahead causes me to sit low on the ground. I am uncertain until I hear a familiar canter through the puddles. It is Petra.

"Good dog. You do not need to come with me. Though I suspect you could protect yourself from the hounds ahead." I pat him on the head and hear someone clear their throat; it is Tata.

"It was a good idea to leave early, Mihnea. Mama had been poking me in the side with 'Let's get up and go!' I guess we all were thinking the same way."

Dumitra stepped up to me, "I mean to be by your side. You cannot sneak off from a huntress. You should know better."

Instead of midday, we would arrive at the castle early in the morn. Maybe the dark would hide some of the sights. The sounds and smells, though in the damp still of the morning, seem loud and overwhelming.

It is not until we near the castle gates I thought fully of what we are doing. Mama is shaking with fear. A camp of soldiers surrounds the castle gates. Swords clang as they practice their skills. I feel some relief as no torture is taking place when we arrive.

I see the rows of dead bodies hung half from the impaling poles on a hill overlooking the castle. We stay together as a group looking poor in our simple garb. I stride out in front and approach the guards.

"Halt! What business do the likes of you have here?" One of the guards looks down from his post.

"I come to speak to my father," I stand solid and squint upward.

The guard leans down with a sneer. "Oh, you do? And who might your father be?"

"Vlad Tepes. Your Master." I see the guard beckon another closer.

They laugh hardily. "Oh, not another claiming to be his bastard son! These poor will do anything to get a stale biscuit!" He spits down towards me.

Another guard leans on his spear. "If your life is worth anything, I suspect it's not, but if it is, you'll turn around and go back from where you came. Dracula does not take lying lightly. You and yours may find yourselves up poles before nightfall."

Dumitra steps up, and before I can stop her, strings her bow with an arrow. "Nobody calls my husband a liar!" She points the arrow straight at the guard.

From the towers, all guards scurry into action. A dozen arrows instantly point in our direction.

A loud growl comes from behind them all. "Halt! Do not let your arrows fly!" Looking over the tower's edge the round man leans almost falling. "It cannot be!" The others follow his orders and lower their weapons. Soon, the gates open, and the older, but always plump, Sir Stefan steps forward.

"Mihnea, could it be you?" The old guard looks at me with a shining smile. Then he steps toward me and we hug and kiss each other on the cheeks.

I nod and tears begin to fall. "Yes, Sir Stefan, I have returned."

"Oh, your father will want to know! I must go to him."

"Sir Stephan, I will go with you." I signal for Dumitra and the others to wait and grab Sir Stephen's arm. "I'll be back shortly."

The two of us hurry through the gate and up a corridor. Sir Stefan must now be of even higher rank. "Let this man through!" All the armed guards bow and obey his order.

We step up the stairs of my childhood. It brings back such memories. Even the smells are the same. Mostly of death, but they are still familiar. I look into the hall and think of my last time there. It was the instant before my mother jumped to her death.

Up the hall to my father's chambers, we go. I quietly follow along with my staff helping me up the steps.

Sir Stefan knocks loudly on the door. "Sir, you have a visitor." He is so jolly he cannot stop his laughter. "One that will surprise you!"

My father's voice growled out as though a bear waken from its winter slumber. "Oh, a visitor, he must be very important for you to come to my chambers so early in the morning." My hood is up as he opens the door and looks out at me. I see the tension in his face and the clenching of his teeth. "Oh, it is a Shepherd. Yes, I am certain he is worthy of my time. Give me a moment."

I move closer as I see the glistening of a sword in my father's hands. His back is to his faithful guard. With nearly the speed I recall, he swirls to lop off Sir Stefan's head.

The instant of his movement, I lift my staff and solidly block the sword. "There will be no killing today!" I shout. My staff is firm causing his sword to shake.

He looks at me like a mad dog about to fight for food. Spittle drops from his gasping mouth and he pants." Who dares to give me an order?" his words echo throughout the castle.

I take down my hood. "It is none other than I. Mihnea, your son. The one you left behind to die in the wilds. I come to ask for help, as it is my right."

He falls back against the wall with his hair in disarray. He wipes his mouth and looks closely again. Blinking again and again. I do not know what awaits me, but I make my silent prayer. It is as though time does not move. He looks at me in a way he never had, it is as though he sees

Dracula's Son

me for the first time as he places his hand on my face. Then he laughs a deep roaring laugh and I regret being there. I have risked all and it may be for nothing. He is silent for a moment. I cannot read his mind, then, "But how can this be? I cannot believe this!" I stand tall and await I know not what. Will he call some more guards to haul me away to the dungeons? Will he be kind enough to hand me a loaf of bread and send me on my way? "Sir Stefan, fetch my steward. We will be having a feast tonight! My son returns just when I need him most! Mihnea, you please your father greatly. I did think you died long ago. We will meet as two men in the courtyard shortly." He pulls me close and kisses me on the cheeks. He must feel the stiffness of my shoulders. I look again at the man who called my mother a bitch and left me to die. I must forgive, but I am full of confusion. I hesitate. Maybe this is one of his humorous traps?

I do not ever remember it so, but my father had some kind of different smile on his face. It struck me as almost kind and with definite humor. It seems strange. Yes, be cautious, I tell myself. Do not trust him. It may be one of his traps!

I walk back down and out the front gate to Dumitra and my family. The word of my return has already spread throughout the castle. The guards who had so recently confronted us each in turn lowered their heads. "Mercy, sir. Mercy, my lady." We stroll together through the gates and towards the courtyard.

This pleases Dumitra, and she stops to stare at the guards, "You are lucky one of my arrows did not pierce your hearts. Never call my husband a liar". Many heads bow again with, "Yes, my lady". Mama spits on the ground at their feet as she prances by.

The main gates are open. Riders head off towards town. We wait in silence on the courtyard benches. I turn and take Tata's hand. "Tata, I asked you to forgive me for my part in not being honest. Now I ask another favor."

"What would that be, Son?" Tata sits silent waiting for my response.

"Can you forgive my true father for what he has done? It would help matters. I do not trust him, but we cannot change the past," I say.

Tata looks at the ground. "I will be honest with your father. This is as God would have it. What he did was wrong. He must know I fear God but I do not fear him. In the end, yes, it is as Christ did, I will forgive him."

I nod though I dread to hear it. How will Dracula react? Bravery is what I need. It is what we all need and love. My strength is love. God will help us. "Yes, you are right, Tata. He is not as great a man as you. Love is the way. I will follow your lead."

We wait silently. I hold Dumitra's hand and Tata holds Mama's.

The air changes. A sudden chill. The guards stand straight and still. Dracula approaches from the far side of the courtyard. He steps near and has his eyes upon us. He turns to some of the servants nearby. "Why do you not make my guest more comfortable? They are my son's family. Get them some water and wine. Now!"

Then Tata walks straight up to my father. They look each other up and down. One in the rich garb of a prince. The other wearing a weather-worn shepherd's cloak. It is simply two men meeting. One has the power of fear and the other of love.

I explain. "This is the man who saved me. His name is Grigore, but I call him Tata. He has been my only father for so long." I step between them. The two looked each other straight in the eyes.

It is silent, and then Dracula speaks. "You have something to share with me?"

"Yes," Tata looks straight at him as an equal and without humility, "I do have something to say to you."

Dracula's Son

All is silent. Even the birds do not sing. My father nods and I find I am sweating with beads trailing down my sides from my armpits.

"You had my true son killed. I now know your son as my own. I have raised him and loved him and guided him in all matters a father should. You must know, though I am a Shepherd, I do not fear you. If you decide to take my new son from me, I only ask this. Take me to."

Then Mama Tudora stood up. "Take me as well."

Then Dumitra stood. "You will also have to take me."

The four of us stood together as one and even Petra came and sat in front of us.

My father looks at the group and laughs. It is not the cruel laugh of old. It is something else. It is, I believe, heartfelt. Impossibly he has tears in his eyes. "The new Prince of this castle has already spoken. He gave me an order 'There will be no killing today'". He looks at me and puts his hand on my shoulder. "Would that I could have raised him to be as strong. I can hardly see myself in him. He is not one to rule as I have. While I am one who has used fear as the mortar for my kingdom, he will not. He has courage—but his rock will be faith and love, not fear. I cannot help that he makes this decision, but I will respect it." Then he turns to me, "Tonight if you accept, I will announce you as the new Prince of this castle. I have a war to fight and have had omens I will not return. God has let me know I need to hand off this castle. My young sons are two sausages and I know they will not be rulers. Their mother is a servant and bows to my every whim. Your mother had another strength. She did not fear me. I am in debt to you and your Mama. I cannot say how this world works, but I do know in my heart you are destined to rule this kingdom. I give it to you."

Then my father turns to Tata. "You will no longer be a poor Shepherd." He reaches toward a nearby advisor takes a scroll from him. He hands this to Tata. "I give this to you. It is as I believe God would have me do. I have already marked off this map giving you the whole of this mountain range. I do not ask for your forgiveness of things I have done, but in honoring truth, I would ask you always be as honest a man. You and your family will have no more worries."

***

It is late in the night when my father introduces me to his help and followers from the village. Each, in turn, approaches to kiss Dumitra's and my hand.

As Matei approaches in tatters of greasy garb with his wife holding the hands of their little boy and girl, I stand. They all kneel. "Please stand," I say. "Matei, my old friend, and so much a brother, I have a question for you."

"Yes. Yes, anything, Master," he responds.

"If you have had enough of the kitchen, I will ask you to accept an appointment to my court. I have the need for your knowledge and stories," I smile at him.

"I quite like the kitchen, but only for the memories," he laughs. "Yes, I will join your court."

We embrace and shed tears. "Thank you, Matei, thank you!" I said. Then to the side, I whisper, "Voicu is still with us," he nods and stepped off to the side.

And the night goes on. Dumitra and I need sleep. Mama and Tata rest at the nearest bench with Petra lying at their feet. There are just a few more to greet.

It is the last in line which surprises us. Lancu approaches with the most fearful look on his face. He jumps down on the floor and sobs, as he holds my ankles. "Please, sir, I meant no harm. Please! Please! Can you forgive me? Please, forgive me!" he pleads. He rolls back and forth kissing my feet and the tears run out of his fearful eyes.

I take his hand and lift him with four words. "Let us be friends."

THE HISTORY MYSTERY GUY

J.W. Keleher

Made in the USA
Columbia, SC
11 April 2025